#Frankenstein

Or,

The Modern Prometheus

#Frankenstein

Or,

The Modern Prometheus

A Literary Classic Told in Tweets
for the 21st-Century Audience

**Based Upon
Frankenstein; Or, The Modern
Prometheus by Mary Shelley**

Abridged & reimagined by
Mike Bezemek

Skyhorse Publishing

Skyhorse Publishing books may be purchased in bulk at special discounts for sales promotion, corporate gifts, fund-raising, or educational purposes. Special editions can also be created to specifications. For details, contact the Special Sales Department, Skyhorse Publishing, 307 West 36th Street, 11th Floor, New York, NY 10018 or info@skyhorsepublishing.com.

Skyhorse® and Skyhorse Publishing® are registered trademarks of Skyhorse Publishing, Inc.®, a Delaware corporation.

Visit our website at www.skyhorsepublishing.com.

10 9 8 7 6 5 4 3 2 1

Library of Congress Cataloging-in-Publication Data is available on file

Jacket artwork: iStockphoto

Print ISBN: 978-1-5107-3134-9
Ebook ISBN: 978-1-5107-3135-6

Printed in the United States of America

To my mom, for a love of writing; to my dad, for a love of reading; and to my brother, for fighting back . . . these tweets are respectfully inscribed.

CONTENTS

ABOUT *FRANKENSTEIN*

Few classic works of literature have excited such enduring popular interest among the general public as the gothic novel *Frankenstein* by Mary Shelley. Even the very origin of its composition carries a gothic mysteriousness as recounted in her introduction to the 1831 edition.

During a rainy June in 1816, also called the "year without a summer," Mary and Percy Blythe Shelley visited Lake Geneva. There, they became neighbors of the famous poet Lord Byron, who was vacationing with friend John William Polidori. Shut inside for days by stormy weather, the four English writers began to read aloud in French from a translated volume of German ghost stories. This gave Lord Byron an idea.

@lordygeorgeordy:
First, man, we know a lot of languages! Second, let's each write a ghost story! Mine's about vampires. #dibs[1]

#Frankenstein; Or, The Modern Prometheus

For Byron's part, he created what became one of the first stories in English to feature a vampire. Byron's incomplete story was later published as "A Fragment of a Novel" in the poetry collection *Mazeppa*. This fragment inspired Polidori to write *The Vampyre* (1819), which is considered the predecessor of the modern vampire genre. And Polidori, in turn, inspired that genre's best-known offering, *Dracula* (1897), by its best-named author, Bram Stoker.

In the days following the challenge, Mary Shelley struggled to imagine a story. Meanwhile, the friends' conversations ranged from Erasmus Darwin's theories of life, to muscle contraction through galvanism, to reanimating corpses, and to potentially, one day, assembling a creature. Soon, Shelley found her idea.

> @reallymaryshelley:
> Couldn't sleep last night, I had the craziest vision. A mad scientist builds a beast, then takes a nap, and gets woke by said beast. #setinwinter[2]

While the others soon abandoned their ghost stories, Shelley's grew into an entire novel. *Frankenstein* was published anonymously in 1818 when Shelley was only twenty years old. From the very beginning, the novel attracted a great deal of attention but received mixed reviews. Many of the negative responses aimed at two primary issues—the author and the monster.

> @sirwalterscott71:
> A wild tale by a logical author! He uses plain English without German hyperbole. But a literate, self-taught monster? Yeah I don't think so.[3]

> @literarypanorama:
> Inconsistent at best! Reanimate dead matter, SURE. But just how does this monster learn to WALK & TALK? Let alone READ! #plotholes[4]

About *Frankenstein*

@edinburghliterary:
The wildest story with an air of reality. But it panders to today's readers with exaggeration and oddity. Readers of today, smh! For them, Shakespeare is boring.[5]

@johnwilsoncroker:
Horrible. Disgusting. Absurd. Appalling. The author? Probs insane. If you read this and liked it? You're probs insane. Only one "praise": #creepy[6]

@thebritishcritic:
WTF is the point? Powerful in spots, but otherwise pointless perversion. We hear the author is a lady? This grotesque nightmare is #notladylike.[7]

Not until publication of the French edition in 1822 did Mary Shelley's name appear as author. And it wasn't until the 2nd English edition of 1831, that Shelley included the introduction described above to answer the question she said she most frequently was asked:

Um, hey @reallymaryshelley. How did a little girl come up with a big mean story like that one? #messedup[8]

For the remainder of her life, Shelley continued to write a variety of books, including the apocalyptic novel *The Last Man* (1826), the historical novel *The Fortunes of Perkin Warbeck* (1830), and the travel book *Rambles in Germany and Italy* (1844). But, similar to the circumstances of her most famous character, Victor Frankenstein, Shelley's life was followed by tragedy. Only one of her three children survived childhood. Her husband, Percy Blythe Shelley drowned in 1822. And during the final decade of her life, Shelley suffered from headaches and paralysis before succumbing at the age of 53 to a suspected brain tumor.

In the years since—and perhaps adding a final insult to her many injuries—Shelley's most famous work has become distorted through countless adaptations and reimaginings (not this one, of course). Today, the name Frankenstein is more commonly associated with the monster, who in most retellings is often portrayed as a numb and mindless animal, not the tortured and contemplative character Shelley created. The doctor, meanwhile, is often portrayed as a noble, if misguided, benefactor.

And those curious bolts on the neck of your typical Halloween Frankenstein costume? Courtesy of the infamous portrayal by Boris Karloff in the 1930s film franchise, which also provided two of the most famous literary misquotes of all time.

> @moviedoktorfrankenstein:
> Oh, it's alive! it's alive! it's alive! . . . HELLO? can everyone hear me? (I always like to repeat myself three or four times.) I said it's ALIVE.

> @frankensteinsmoviemonster:
> ERRrrrrrrrrrrr . . . . . . ERrrrrr . . .? (Always got my arms up, but never can get a hug.) . . . Errrr . . . . . .

DISCLAIMER

The contents of this book—tweets, hashtags, taglines, handles, etc.—are a product of the author's imagination and are in no way affiliated with Twitter or any of its users. This book is not authorized or sponsored by Twitter, Inc., or any other person or entity owning or controlling rights in the Twitter name, trademark, or copyrights.

#Frankenstein
or,
The Modern Prometheus

INTRODUCTION

@reallymaryshelley:

My husband didn't write this book. I wrote this book. #duh
#hedidencouragemetho[9]

THE TWEETS

@captainrobwalton:

Hello from St. Petersburgh! Six years planning and I'm finally taking a sledge to the Archangelsk port. The icy northern breeze excites me! (#shite, did I pack my furs?)[10]

♥ 🗨 ↻ ≡

I seek to visit wild seas and eternal sun, hit up an unvisited pole, find the northwest passage, and discover what wondrous power attracts the needle! Back in a few years (or never). 💀 #dreamtrip[11]

♥ 🗨 ↻ ≡

3

My ship and crew are hired, now we wait for spring. I may be a romantic, but I wish I had a buddy to share the voyage with. Doubt I'll meet peeps in the Arctic.[12]

Already we've reached a very high latitude over pathless seas! Ice sheets float past. Please recall me with affection if I don't return. (FYI—no incidents so far.) #allgood[13]

The ship is stuck in ice and fog—WTF! A dogsled just sped across the ice, heading north. It was driven by a giant being shaped like a man?! Damn. I thought I was first up here. #bummer[14]

It's morning, and the sea has finally broken—are you EFFing kidding me? Another guy just floated up on an ice raft! A Swiss sled driver, half-frozen and emaciated. Says he's only coming aboard if we're going north?! #notmanyoptionspal[15]

My new bud improves daily, but he's always watching the sea for the "demon" on that first sled. Says he was a slave to passion. By great misfortune he lost all but grief. He's gonna share his tale![16]

♥   💬   ↻   ≡

@frankendoctorvictor:

I'll start at the beginning. (Like the very beginning, cool?) My ancestors were top Geneva lawyers and judges. My pop worked for the government. #mylifewasaight[17]

♥   💬   ↻   ≡

Pop had a buddy in Lucerne (with a daughter) go broke and die from depression. #happens. So, Pop married the daughter (my mom!) and had a #maydecemberthing.[18]

♥   💬   ↻   ≡

'Til age five I was the only child. The IDOL of my folks. The smelter to their mine of hearts. The tassel on their silk cord. The engineer on our happy fam train. #igotmore #holdmybeer[19]

♥   💬   ↻   ≡

We traveled ALL the time! Germany, France, Italy. My folks luved to visit the poor. At Lake Como, mom met a cute orphan girl named Liz. Not Italian, but a #BLOND. 😜 20

Mom adopted Liz, and surprised Pop and me. She said Liz was my gift! We called each other "cuz." (But I was like, "gonna tap that someday.") #putaringonit[21]

The folks spoiled us with a lake house. Liz loved Swiss mountains and seasons. My pal Henry loved playing King Arthur. And I loved the occult. #gofigure[22]

I read wild fancies of discredited alchemists: raising ghosts and demons! Elixirs of life! Immortality! ⚖ Such fatal impulses led to my ruin . . . [23]

. . . plus an accident! Lightning struck our oak tree, reducing it to ribbons of wood. Electricity? Galvanism? I abandoned alchemy for math. #geeklife[24]

❤ 💬 ↻ ≡

While prepping to leave for college, my first misfortune struck. Mom caught scarlet fever from Liz and calmly died. Liz resolved to care for the family.[25]

❤ 💬 ↻ ≡

How excited I was to arrive at Ingolstadt University! But my natural philosophy professor was a total jerk. 😢 He talked all kinds of shit. #ahole[26]

❤ 💬 ↻ ≡

@herrproffesordoktorkrempe:

Sweet Jesus! 1000-year-old alchemists? You've wasted years, Herr Frankincense. Pull your head out of the sand. This is the enlightened age. #dolt[27]

❤ 💬 ↻ ≡

@frankendoctorvictor:

I was like #whatevs. Sniff, sniff (got something in my eye). I was already done with them alchemy fools. Luckily, I found a way better prof. #myfav[28]

♥   🗨   ↻   ≡

@professorwallywaldman:

Those ancient teachers promised the impossible, but did nada. Modern masters promise little, but perform miracles. Microscopes! Circulation! Oxygenation! #otherstuff[29]

♥   🗨   ↻   ≡

But us modern scholars are indebted to those founders' zeal. Genius erroneously directed is still genius. Study all the sciences, Vic. #yesmath2[30]

♥   🗨   ↻   ≡

@frankendoctorvictor:

For years, I didn't visit Geneva. I did nothing but lab science—chem, anatomy, physiology. I sought a bold discovery: the secret to life. #nbd[31]

♥   🗨   ↻   ≡

But first, I had to figure out death. I spent nights in vaults with skeletons, in graveyards watching bodies decay and worms eating brains. 🥄 You know, #fieldtrips![32]

♥   💬   ↻   ☰

One dark night, a light came on. All before me had failed, yet I discovered the simple secret to bestowing life! (I'd prefer not to share.) #handsoff #dangerousdeets[33]

♥   💬   ↻   ☰

I wondered, what should I make? No silly animal—I went straight to a human with muscles and veins. I'm talkin' a giant, like 8 feet tall with shoes off. #gotcocky[34]

♥   💬   ↻   ☰

FYI, it takes A LOT of effort to become the father to a new species and maybe one day cure the dying! I lost A LOT of weight. #beachbod[35]

♥   💬   ↻   ☰

I worked nights collecting body parts from damp graves, slaughterhouses, and dissecting rooms. May have tortured a few animals. (Got super #lockedin.)[36]

Four seasons passed while shut in my attic workshop. I caught a fever. Falling leaves made me #freakout. Plus, carrying body parts upstairs? First floor lab is better. [37]

I forgot my family and never wrote. Beware of such obsessions! They killed the Greeks, Romans, Mayans, Aztecs, American Indians . . . #coolyourjets[38]

A rainy November night, under a dying candle, I infused the spark. A gasp! A convulsion of limbs! A yellow eye opened WTF had I done?[39]

Yellow skin (I really ♥ yellow btw) stretched over muscles, plus black lips and hair. I shoulda thought this thru more. Dude was #fugly.[40]

♥　　💬　　↻　　≡

For two years, I'd toiled, but now all hopes for beauty turned to horror and disgust. #smh. I rushed from the lab to my bed and passed out. Slept to the wildest dreams. . . [41]

♥　　💬　　↻　　≡

. . . I saw Liz and kissed her—NO! She turned into my mother's corpse, crawling with worms and wearing flannel. (Seriously—flannel?!) #nightmare[42]

♥　　💬　　↻　　≡

I awoke to the miserable monster hovering at my bedside, jaws gaping in a grin. He reached for me—but I ran to the courtyard and paced the streets 'til morning. #closecall[43]

♥　　💬　　↻　　≡

I tried to forget; recited some lite poetry; considered moving. A coach pulled up and parked in front of me. The door opened, and a passenger jumped out. #kindabusyrightnow[44]

Oh hey @kinghenryclerval! What a surprise! So great to see you! Anywho, my place is SUCH a mess! Let me clean up real quick! Back in a sec![45]

I ran upstairs and threw open the door. The place was empty. No hideous house guest, not even a ghost. #luckybreak[46]

Ok, come on up, @kinghenryclerval! No big haps here, lol! Let's have breakfast! I created a monster, hahahaha!—I mean, no I didn't. #longnight[47]

@kinghenryclerval:

Um . . . are you alright, @frankendoctorvictor? Sorry to come spur of the moment. I was accepted at the Uni. Why are you laughing so much? #ubeendrinkin?[48]

♥ 💬 ↻ ≡

@frankendoctorvictor:

I fell into a delirium for months, saw the monster errrywhere. Poor Henry cared for me as I raved mad. But by spring I was cool. #allgood[49]

♥ 💬 ↻ ≡

@kinghenryclerval:

Hey @frankendoctorvictor, my main man. Now that you're better, I really gotta ask you something . . . [50]

♥ 💬 ↻ ≡

@frankendoctorvictor:

Um . . . ok @kinghenryclerval . . . fire away. So, is it like a math question or something?[51]

♥ 💬 ↻ ≡

@kinghenryclerval:

When the heck are you going to message your dad and cousin? They must be super worried![52]

@frankendoctorvictor:

Oh phew—I mean . . . oh YOU—oh YOU are so right, my bro from another mo! I forgot about my fam! In fact, I think my cuz sent me a ton of messages while I was sick.[53]

@lizziefromthelake:

My dear @frankendoctorvictor, I was so happy to hear FROM HENRY that you're better. I have so much to tell you. I'll start at the beginning. (Like the very beginning, ok?)[54]

Well, the mountains are still snowy, and the lake's still blue, and the kids are still growing, and the house is still standing, FYI.[55]

Ernie is sixteen now and waaay outdoorsy—a true Swiss. He's joining the foreign service (never liked to read), and your dad's not crazy about it. #thatkid[56]

❤   💬   ↻   ≡

Remember Justine Moritz? Your favorite maid? Her dad, brothers, sister all tragically died? Joined us at age 12 and was sooo polite? (She got super HOT.) #seriously[57]

❤   💬   ↻   ≡

And your brother, little William! He's five now and not so little anymore, with blue eyes, dark lashes, curly hair, dimples. Has tons of crushes. #playa[58]

❤   💬   ↻   ≡

Meanwhile, EVERYONE is getting married: pretty Miss Mansfield, her uggo sis, your pal Louis. 😒 #whatevs #nonewsaboutme #dropmealine[59]

❤   💬   ↻   ≡

@*frankendoctorvictor:*

Hey @lizziefromthelake! I'm way better now. Test tubes still make me gag, but otherwise good. Thanks for the messages! #youdabest[60]

♥   💬   ↻   ≡

For the next two years, I finished my studies. Got a new apartment. Chilled with Clerv and kept delaying a trip home until one day I heard from Pop.[61]

♥   💬   ↻   ≡

@*frankalphonstein:*

Son, I'm so sorry to deliver this news. @frankendoctorvictor, your little brother William has died. Murdered. Strangled on a hike in the Alps. We are beyond crushed.[62]

♥   💬   ↻   ≡

But Liz is even worse. She blames herself for letting Viktor wear that pricey pendant with your mom's pic. It was stolen by the murderer. #pleasecomehome[63]

♥   💬   ↻   ≡

@frankendoctorvictor:

Distraught, I traveled for home but first crossed the lake to where William was killed. Lightning played upon Mont Blanc as a storm descended upon the spot.[64]

♥ 💬 ↻ ≣

"Oh, William!" I cried on the hilltop. Then, in flashes, I saw a figure amid the trees. A giant? The filthy daemon I had made? He was the murderer! #shit[65]

♥ 💬 ↻ ≣

The depraved wretch scrambled through mist. He had destroyed my bro! Another flash and this devil climbed cliffs to the summit and vanished. #thisonme[66]

♥ 💬 ↻ ≣

After a night of misery, I ran to town. I had to tell all! I'd made a murderous beast during delirious college dayz! Last seen on a sheer mountain at midnight . . . [67]

♥ 💬 ↻ ≣

. . . (VERY sorry!) But we must pursue and kill it! As I approached the town, I had second thoughts. Who gonna believe that? #betterkeepquiet[68]

♥   💬   ↻   ≡

@ernestthefrankest:

Hey, @frankendoctorvictor. When are you coming over, bro? Liz is losing it since they caught the murderer. (They caught the murderer, btw.)[69]

♥   💬   ↻   ≡

@frankendoctorvictor:

NO WAY! @ernestthefrankest, who could chase him? That's like catching the wind. Or damming a mountain stream with straw. I saw the dude last night. #doubtit[70]

♥   💬   ↻   ≡

@ernestthefrankest:

Ok, not sure what that all means, @frankendoctorvictor, but it was a SHE, actually. Justine Moritz. There's a bunch of evidence. Justine #sux . . .[71]

♥   💬   ↻   ≡

. . . to review: 1) She had a pendant with mom's pic in her pocket the day after William was murdered. 2) She acted way suspicious. 3) Um, see points 1 & 2. #throwawaythekey[72]

♥   🗩   ↻   ≡

@frankendoctorvictor:

Justine Moritz? Were they all nuts? I went to see Liz and assured her there was no way for a conviction. #insanity. So, I figured, why make my horror story public? 🤚 [73]

♥   🗩   ↻   ≡

At the trial, more "facts" came out. Justine was away the whole night of the murder and was seen the next morning near the crime scene. When she saw the body? Got way emotional. #trippin[74]

♥   🗩   ↻   ≡

Justine swore innocence and told her story: Coming back from her aunt's house, Justine heard William was missing. She went to search and was locked outside Geneva's gates . . .[75]

♥   🗩   ↻   ≡

. . . Justine spent the night in a neighbor's barn, woke from footsteps, and went outside to search. She had no idea how the pendant, with mom's pic, got into her pocket. #framed?[76]

Liz spoke on Justine's behalf. But to NO effect. The public and judges were convinced. The ballots were cast. Guilty and condemned. #ohcrap[77]

@lizziefromthelake:

I can't believe it, @frankendoctorvictor. We both thought she was innocent, but now they say @justthemaidmoritz confessed! #howcouldshe?[78]

@justthemaidmoritz:

Oh, @lizziefromthelake, I confessed a lie! They called me a monster, threatened hell and fire, offered me absolution in exchange. Please believe me, #iluvedbeingyourmaid. 🖐[79]

The Tweets

@frankendoctorvictor:

I couldn't reply. The daemon that I'd made had killed. And framed an innocent to die for its crimes. The next morning, Justine hung on the scaffold, a murderess. Two victims #myfault.[80]

♥ 💬 ↻ ≡

Hence forth, I felt only remorse, guilt, and a desire for vengeance. My Pop grieved and consoled me. Liz cried and begged me to let my anger go. #iftheyonlyknew[81]

♥ 💬 ↻ ≡

I floated nights on the lake, drifting with the wind. Waited for the monster's next awful crime. (Recited some lite poetry.) Roamed the Alps for distraction. #hurtin[82]

♥ 💬 ↻ ≡

One day, I climbed to Montanvert glacier and stood atop a river of ice. I stared at peaks glittering with sunlight and felt the first tinges of joy in months. #thingslookinup[83]

♥ 💬 ↻ ≡

In the distance, I saw a huge figure approaching. The unearthly wretch! I took a swing, but he ducked aside. "Devil!" I raged. "Vile insect!" #notalooker[84]

@iamnotttamonstar:

Calm down and hear me out, @frankendoctorvictor. You may be my creator, but you made me bigger and stronger. #greatbonestructure #icouldkickurass[85]

@frankendoctorvictor:

Ok . . . um . . . didn't expect that, @iamnotttamonstar. But are you shitting me? I oughta trample you to dust. Extinguish your spark. #uwereamistake[86]

@iamnotttamonstar:

Don't be SUCH an ass, @frankendoctorvictor. Listen to my story. I'll start at the beginning. The VERY beginning. (Or I'll kill everyone you know.) #toughchoice #youSOoweme[87]

My senses were raw at first. Everything was dark and opaque, then bright and overwhelming. I sought shade in a forest by Ingolstadt. I ate berries and drank from a creek. #notapicnic[88]

My senses were raw at first. Everything was dark and opaque, then bright and overwhelming. I sought shade in a forest by Ingolstadt. I ate berries and drank from a creek. #notapicnic[88]

Under the night orb, I felt cold—despite taking clothes from your apartment. (Thanks, btw. #tightfit) Then I found a huge cloak under a tree. #newthreads[89]

I felt the warmth of an abandoned fire. Tasted meat, smelled the forest, heard pretty songs by the winged animals. I tried to mimic, but failed. #cantwhistle[90]

One night, it snowed. The next morning, I sought shelter at a small hut. When I entered, an old man saw me and freaked the F out. #hebolted[91]

I downed his bread, milk, cheese, wine, and fell asleep. (First #foodcoma.) Nearby, I found a village and they all freaked the F out, too. #seeingapatternhere[92]

Children shrieked and women fainted. Some fled, some attacked. I learned about: brooms, hammers, pitchforks, and stones (specifically, the throwing of). #ouch[93]

I escaped to the countryside and took refuge in a dry hovel next to a cottage. The family inside included a blind father, a son, and daughter. #theywascool[94]

Through a hole, I observed. The family was poor and hungry, but so kind. The son collected wood and tended garden. The daughter milked a cow and cooked. The father played guitar. #hippies [95]

I longed to join them, but dared not. Overheard sounds which I discovered were words. Slowly, I learned language. Turns out I'm #waysmart. 🐵 #whoknew[96]

I ♥   💬   ↻   ≡

Each night, I collected firewood and left it on their doorstep. Foraging for my food, I once saw my face in moonlit water. #woah #yikes #okigetitnow[97]

♥   💬   ↻   ≡

The family spoke of me as a "wonderful spirit." But they were still sad despite my help. I felt such funny new feelings, and I cried for my protectors. #superbummed[98]

♥   💬   ↻   ≡

One day, Safie arrived, a beautiful young woman with raven-black hair. The son was so #stoked. Soon, I learned the cottagers' history. (FYI—I'll start at the beginning, alright?) #fromthetop[99]

♥   💬   ↻   ≡

@frankendoctorvictor:

Gee, that would be great, @iamnotttamonstar. #yawn #greatstuff[100]

❤   💬   ↻   ≡

@iamnotttamonstar:

Ok, so Old DeLacey was a rich Frenchman and father to Agatha and Felix. They lived in Paris— HEY! @frankendoctorvictor. Are you nodding off? #keepittogetherman[101]

❤   💬   ↻   ≡

@frankendoctorvictor:

Huh . . . what? Me? No, no. Please continue. #justrestingmyeyes

❤   💬   ↻   ≡

@iamnotttamonstar:

As I was explaining, Safie's dad was a Turkish merchant. Because of his religion, he was sentenced unfairly to die. Felix heard about this and came to the trial . . . [102]

❤   💬   ↻   ≡

. . . and when Felix saw Safie, it was all 💙💙💙. He figured why not help the father and maybe win the daughter? So Felix hatched an escape plan.[103]

The three of them escaped to Italy, but the French government found out and arrested DeLacey and Agatha. Next, the Turk took Safie away from Felix. #dadblock[104]

The government left the family penniless and exiled to the cottage. But Safie loved Felix, so she escaped from her dad and came to find her man. #sweetstory #seethatwasworthit[105]

Meanwhile, I turned one year old #inmyhole. I scavenged books about nations, wars, murders, money, religion, and suicide. #factsRdepressing[106]

I had your lab coat with notes on my creation. Now I could read: "hateful day," "hideous wretch," "frightful fiend," "demon corpse". . . [107]

. . . um, "Not even Satan would befriend," "could make Dante puke," "I'd rather bang a mummy than look at that thing"?! #btdubs #urprettymeanbruh[108]

I decided to meet the cottagers. So nice and happy now that Safie had arrived, surely they could overlook my deformities. (Plus, I brought firewood.) #gotthehookup[109]

One winter day, blind DeLacey sat by the fire. I knocked and entered. We chatted of origins, not having any friends, that whole me-being-a-monster thing. #2peasinapod[110]

DeLacey was SO cool. #thebest. But the others came back early and freaked the F out. Agatha fainted, Safie split, and Felix beat me with a stick. I ran into the woods and sobbed. 😭 #hurtin[111]

DeLacey was SO cool. #thebest. But the others came back early and freaked the F out. Agatha fainted, Safie split, and Felix beat me with a stick. I ran into the woods and sobbed.

I wanted to kill and destroy, but not my friends. By the next morning, they were gone—moved away. I howled with rage, burned the cottage, vowed war with man. 🔥 #lookwhatyoumademedo[112]

Where to next? Why, to you, @frankendoctorvictor. Only my creator might offer me pity and justice—or vengeance. (Everything's on the table.) Your notes mentioned Geneva. #roadtrip![113]

I traveled mostly at night. But in the mountains, beauty drew me into the open. I rescued a little girl swept into a stream. Got shot by her dad for my troubles. #Rukiddingme?[114]

Nearing Geneva at dusk, I approached a sweet boy. He called me "OGRE." Said his dad, Alphonse Frankenstein, was a "big deal." (So yeah, I strangled him.) #sueme[115]

I took his pendant with a pic of a pretty lady. Hiding in a nearby barn, I saw a beautiful young woman sleeping, and I slipped it into her pocket. Why? Because #shewouldneverdateme[116]

Now, I've found you, @frankendoctorvictor, and here's my request. NO, my demand. Make me a companion of the same species with the same defects. And don't forget the #ladyparts. [117]

@frankendoctorvictor:

Um . . . no thanks, @iamnotttamonstar.[118]

p.s. 'cause you ARE a monster. (Clever speaker, sure, I'll give you that. #praisedue) But why would I make a second monster? #yeahright[119]

@*iamnotttamonstar:*

Ok 1) you're wrong 2) I kill because I'm shunned and miserable 3) this is ALL your fault 4) I got real passion for revenge when wronged. #gogetter[120]

. . . 5) if I don't get some luvin, I'm gonna kick some serious ass (#thatbeyou) 6) also your peeps 7) did I mention you'll regret being born?[121]

. . . oh 8) me and my #galpal will stay away from humans 9) we'll go to South America, eat nuts and berries and sleep on dried leaves. #notavaycay #amigettinthru?[122]

@frankendoctorvictor:

Alright, alright. I give in, OK? I guess I do owe you (plus, to spare humanity, etc). But you are soooo out of Europe. #exiled[123]

♥ 💬 ↻ ≡

@iamnotttamonstar:

#Deal[124]

♥ 💬 ↻ ≡

Ok, look, I'm gonna get out of here and let you get back to work. Once you're done, I'll appear. In the meantime, I'll be #watchingyou.[125]

♥ 💬 ↻ ≡

@frankendoctorvictor:

The beast dropped down the mountain like an eagle. I descended slowly, contemplating my task. Making a female would take months. #chicksRcomplicated[126]

♥ 💬 ↻ ≡

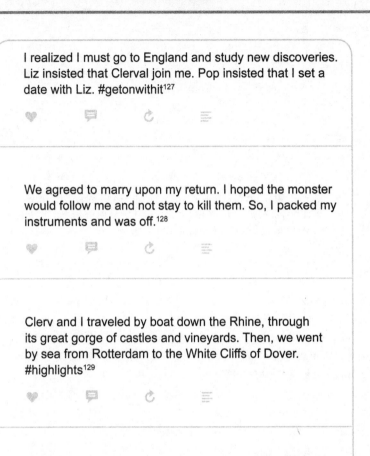

I realized I must go to England and study new discoveries. Liz insisted that Clerval join me. Pop insisted that I set a date with Liz. #getonwithit[127]

We agreed to marry upon my return. I hoped the monster would follow me and not stay to kill them. So, I packed my instruments and was off.[128]

Clerv and I traveled by boat down the Rhine, through its great gorge of castles and vineyards. Then, we went by sea from Rotterdam to the White Cliffs of Dover. #highlights[129]

In London several months, I studied for my new creation (plus collected my "materials." ). Next, we moved onward through England toward Scotland. #worktrip[130]

Each new place was Clerv's favorite, #easy2please, but I was moody and distracted. The fiend was out there and I was neglecting my promise. #quitstallin[131]

I split off from Clerv and sailed to a small island in the Orkneys. On a desolate rock with three huts, I established my basic laboratory. #justthebasics[132]

Each day was more horrible than the last. My first experiment was an enthusiastic frenzy. This second time was cold and sickening. #gotoldfast[133]

I stared at the ground, hoping not to see the beast. This new female creature progressed rapidly, and I began to have doubts.[134]

What if the new beast was 10,000 times worse than the first? What if they hated each other? What if she dumped him for a way hotter guy? #monsterdatingprobz[135]

💜   💬   ↻   ≡

Or worse, suppose they had kids? A race of devils? Threatening all humanity! And me the cause! #badgrandpa[136]

💜   💬   ↻   ≡

Into the moonlit window came the treacherous daemon, with a ghastly grin. Trembling with anger, I tore his hopes to shreds. He howled in despair and left. #rejected[137]

💜   💬   ↻   ≡

I locked the lab and vowed never to resume such work. I sat in my apartment and stared at the sea. I heard a boat rowing outside the window. Waited for his response.[138]

💜   💬   ↻   ≡

@iamnotttamonstar:

What. The. Hell. @frankendoctorvictor?! I crept along the Rhine, hid in cold caves, slept in willows and bogs. F'ing bogs, man. #youburnedme #youblow[139]

You may be my creator, but I am your master. I'll bite you like a venomous snake until you curse the sun. I will be with you on your wedding night. #peaceout[140]

@frankendoctorvictor:

My wedding night! Kill ME on MY wedding night? Not if I kill you first, @iamnotttamonstar. #yourecold #youreawretch #yourenevergettingmarried[141]

The villain's boat shot across the waves like an arrow toward the mainland. I should have followed him and fought to the death, but didn't. #ohwell[142]

I gathered up the half-finished creature, whose parts scattered the lab floor like a mangled human. Put them in a basket with heavy stones.[143]

I took a skiff and sailed under moonlight into the sea. Dropped the basket overboard (#bonvoyage). I hadn't slept in days, so I fixed the rudder and took a #powernap.[144]

I awoke mid-morning, lost at sea! (Had I done the fiend's task and doomed myself? #thatslacker) I sailed blindly until I spotted land. Beached near a town, as a crowd gathered.[145]

"Hey, ya'll!" I said. "Where am I?" "Oh, you'll find out," replied a guy. "Not gonna like it. You're going to jail, dude. You're a murderer."[146]

The facts were relayed. A dry warm body was found near my landing spot. The black mark of fingers on his neck. #wellshit[147]

The magistrate took me to see the body. NO! My pal, Clerv, lifeless and cold. What had I done? I screamed and collapsed. #kindamything[148]

For two months, I lay in prison near death, raving mad and nightmarish. Why didn't I die? (Must have strong heart.) #doomed2live[149]

The magistrate came and declared my innocence from new evidence. The trial would soon exonerate me. In the meantime, a "friend" was coming to visit. #uhoh[150]

@frankalphonstein:

My son, @frankendoctorvictor, a wretched fatality pursues you. And poor Henry, #RIP. Soon I will take you home. #myboy[151]

♥   🗩   ↻   ≡

@frankendoctorvictor:

My pop and I sailed homeward, to my horrible destiny. My cup o' life was poisoned. I saw only darkness pierced by two yellow eyes. #ihateyellow[152]

♥   🗩   ↻   ≡

Overland through Paris, we continued and so did my nightmares. I chowed down on sleeping pills, raved to Pop that I was an assassin. He thought I was #waycray.[153]

♥   🗩   ↻   ≡

@lizziefromthelake:

Heard you'll be home soon, @frankendoctorvictor. You poor thing, I'll take good care of you. But there's something we gotta talk about first.[154]

♥   🗩   ↻   ≡

We've been engaged for like 4eva—like since we were kids, practically. I'm up for this, but are you? Is there someone else? #feetdragging[155]

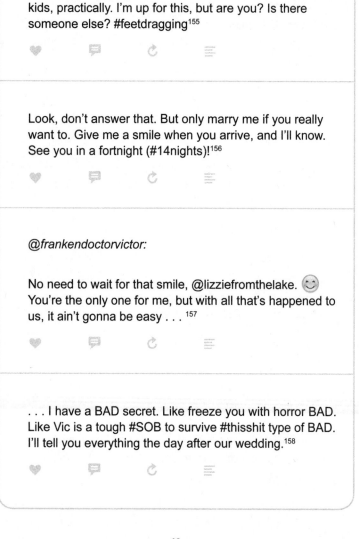

Look, don't answer that. But only marry me if you really want to. Give me a smile when you arrive, and I'll know. See you in a fortnight (#14nights)![156]

@frankendoctorvictor:

No need to wait for that smile, @lizziefromthelake. 🙂 You're the only one for me, but with all that's happened to us, it ain't gonna be easy . . . [157]

. . . I have a BAD secret. Like freeze you with horror BAD. Like Vic is a tough #SOB to survive #thisshit type of BAD. I'll tell you everything the day after our wedding.[158]

The Tweets

Arriving home, I doubted I'd reach the big day. "Be with you on your wedding night?" I no longer feared death by the fiend, but I couldn't let Liz get away. #shemine[159]

♥　　🖻　　↻　　☰

Our wedding day arrived! I carried pistols and dagger. Liz seemed down in the dumps. Maybe that whole hubbie has a BAD secret thing? #thisonme[160]

♥　　🖻　　↻　　☰

Good morning, @lizziefromthelake! Try to cheer up, just for today? (If you knew what I've gone through, you'd do it just for me.) #please?[161]

♥　　🖻　　↻　　☰

@lizziefromthelake:

FYI, just because I'm not smiling doesn't mean I'm unhappy. @frankendoctorvictor, I do have a funny feeling, but #allisgood. . . .[162]

♥　　🖻　　↻　　☰

. . . and it is a beautiful day, I'll give you that. Blue skies and a clear lake. I can see fish swimming on the bottom! Plus, Mont Blanc? #yay #imtryin #frankensteins4eva![163]

♥   💬   ↻   ≡

@frankendoctorvictor:

After the ceremony and reception, Liz and I went by sailboat to a lakeside inn. From the window, I watched night descend with a storm—kept my hand on my gun.[164]

♥   💬   ↻   ≡

I realized my fight with the beast would be way too scary for Liz (plus bloody, btw), so I slyly suggested she go to bed first. #chivalry #willconsumatelater[165]

♥   💬   ↻   ≡

I paced the passages of the inn, searched every corner for my enemy. But I saw no trace. Suddenly, I heard a shrill and deadly SCREAM. #imaketerribledecisions[166]

♥   💬   ↻   ≡

The Tweets

I rushed to our room. The purest creature on earth lay lifeless and inanimate. Thrown across the bed, her head was hanging, and her neck bore the mark of the fiend's grasp.[167]

In the window was the abhorred monster. With a jeering grin, he hideously pointed at Liz's corpse. I fired my pistol as he leaped into the lake.[168]

A crowd gathered and we took boats to search the lake. We cast nets, but in vain. I returned to the room and wept over my wife's body. #misery[169]

I suddenly realized that Pop and Ernest might already be strangled, so I hired a boat, and we rowed upwind toward home. I arrived in time, but still too late.[170]

One by one, all who I ever loved were snatched from me (because of me). Willy. Justine. Clerv. Liz. And Pop. (He died in my arms upon the news.)[171]

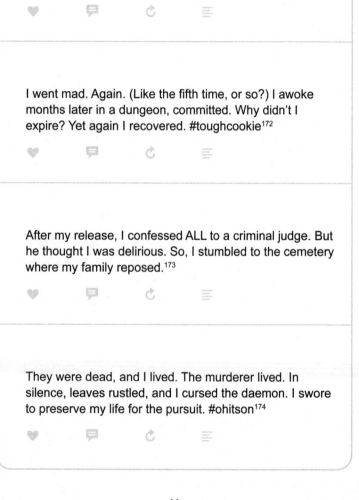

I went mad. Again. (Like the fifth time, or so?) I awoke months later in a dungeon, committed. Why didn't I expire? Yet again I recovered. #toughcookie[172]

After my release, I confessed ALL to a criminal judge. But he thought I was delirious. So, I stumbled to the cemetery where my family reposed.[173]

They were dead, and I lived. The murderer lived. In silence, leaves rustled, and I cursed the daemon. I swore to preserve my life for the pursuit. #ohitson[174]

The Tweets

I would execute my dear #revenge. Make him drink #sweetagony. Meet him in #mortalcombat. Then, in the stillness of night, I heard a loud and fiendish laugh. #thisdudeistoomuch[175]

@okayimamonster:

Alright, @frankendoctorvictor. Let's call it even. I'm satisfied. You're a miserable wretch, but determined to live. #wecool #evensteven[176]

@frankendoctorvictor:

Since that night, I've traversed a vast portion of the earth. Guided by clues, I followed the windings of the Rhône River to the blue Mediterranean. #idoluvtraveling[177]

I followed the fiend aboard a vessel to the Black Sea and into Russia. Peasants pointed me toward his path. Other times I found marks he left.[178]

Cursed by the devil, yet aided by some spirit. Parched by thirst, I'd find water in the desert. Near starving, food awaited me in the wilderness.[179]

Only sleep gave me joy. I saw my home, friends, Clerv, pop, wife—I heard Liz's silver voice. I told myself they were real and that daytime was the dream. #mynightmare[180]

@okayimamonster:

My reign is not yet over, @frankendoctorvictor. As you live, my power is complete. I've left food for you up ahead. Follow close . . .[181]

. . . we have yet to wrestle for our lives. You've got HOURS of misery left. FYI, you better pick up some furs and snacks before the final leg of our journey . . . [182]

. . . your sufferings will satisfy my eternal hatred. You are gonna be SO cold. I seek everlasting ices of the north. #seeyouthere[183]

@frankendoctorvictor:

Dude, quit scoffing, @okayimamonster. You SUCK so MUCH. I am going to torture you. At least when I die, I will join peeps that love me. #thanxforallthetips[184]

The snows thickened, temps dropped, and rivers froze. I bought a sledge and dogs, gained ground on the beast until I was only one day behind. #soclose[185]

At the coast, locals said a giant passed through last night. (No big deal up here, I guess?) And it had guns. After stealing food and sledge, it journeyed out across the frozen sea.[186]

Days of misery passed after I left land—perhaps weeks. The dogs died. I closed within one mile before the ice broke and I rafted away. #cantcatchabreak[187]

I saw your ship at anchor, @captainrobwalton. I broke my sledge into oars and rowed through the night. But if you were going south, I wasn't coming aboard. #icanswim4it[188]

If I die, promise me one thing, @captainrobwalton. Kill the thing. He speaks a good game, but don't trust him. #stabthefool[189]

@captainrobwalton:

Ok, wow. That story is like an erupting volcano, @frankendoctorvictor. That is going to freak the shit out of @margewalton. (Hey, sis!) #wowza[190]

All seems pretty legit, btw. But will you tell me how the creature was built? I don't need a "recipe." #justbasics[191]

♥   💬   ↻   ≣

@frankendoctorvictor:

Are you crazy, my good friend, @captainrobwalton? Are you going to whip up another monster in the galley? Are you not going to learn from me? #listenbuddy[192]

♥   💬   ↻   ≣

When I was young, I had a vivid imagination, cool judgment, and lofty ambitions. I thought myself destined for greatness. #humbletoo[193]

♥   💬   ↻   ≣

Looking back, sure, I was exceptional. I created a sensitive and rational man (er, animal). And thereby I chained myself to eternal HELL. #sux2beme[194]

♥   💬   ↻   ≣

@captainrobwalton:

A sharp fellow, that Frankenstein. Glorious in good days, noble and godlike in ruin. Oh, I should mention that our ship is stuck in ice. (May be crushed any moment.) Crew is pretty pissed. #mutiny?[195]

♥   🗩   ↻   ≡

The cold is severe. Many comrades have succumbed to their desolate graves. The remaining crew demands retreat, meanwhile Frankenstein is near death. #Mondays[196]

♥   🗩   ↻   ≡

@frankendoctorvictor:

Retreat? WTF, guys! Abandon @captainrobwalton and your glorious expedition for honor? Do you miss warm firesides? Your hearts are hot enough to melt ice. #manup[197]

♥   🗩   ↻   ≡

Sure, I owed my creation some happiness. But the guy was malignantly selfish. I was right to refuse him a lady. (And chase him around trying to kill him.) #sorrynotsorry[198]

♥   🗩   ↻   ≡

And yes, avoiding ambition and seeking happiness and tranquility is smarter, but you know which I think is better. I am not going south. #dropmeoff[199]

@captainrobwalton:

The ice broke earlier, but otherwise a bad day. My men turned the ship south, shamefully terminating my voyage. They care nothing for glory or honor. #snowflakes[200]

And Victor Frankenstein died. A glorious spirit was extinguished. I left his body and retired to my cabin to weep—then, I heard a strange voice from Frankenstein's cabin.[201]

Holy. Shit. Inside the cabin was a giant—with ragged hair, skin like a mummy, and hideous face—grieving over the body. He sprung for the window, but I called him to stay.[202]

@okayimamonster:

My final victim. My crimes and being are complete. Oh, Frankenstein, I destroyed you through all that you loved. Will you pardon me? #rhetoricalquestion[203]

♥   💬   ↻   ≡

He suffered not one ten-thousandth that I did. Don't think, @captainrobwalton, that my victim's cries were music to my ears. I abhor myself. I was a slave to evil, not the master. #letsgetreal[204]

♥   💬   ↻   ≡

I once sought love and sympathy, but I received only hatred and misery. A fallen angel turned to a malignant devil. I have only one task left.[205]

♥   💬   ↻   ≡

On an ice raft, I will seek the northern-most pole. (Yep, I'm gonna be first up there.) I'll build my funeral pyre (I brought my own wood) and ascend triumphantly.[206]

♥   💬   ↻   ≡

Farewell, humans. Farewell, sun, stars, and wind. Farewell, remorse, wounds, my miserable frame. Farewell to my ashes, swept into the sea. #poeticAF[207]

♥   💬   ↻   ≡

And farewell, Frankenstein. I am going to burn myself to death. I'm kinda #dramatic like that.[208]

♥   💬   ↻   ≡

APPENDIX

Endnotes

1   Author's Introduction, 1831 edition. "'We will each write a ghost story,' said Lord Byron; and his proposition was acceded to."

2   Author's Introduction, 1831 edition. "When I placed my head on my pillow, I did not sleep . . . I saw the pale student of unhallowed arts kneeling beside the thing he had put together. I saw the hideous phantasm of a man stretched out . . . show signs of life . . . His success would terrify the artist; he would rush away from his odious handywork, horror-stricken . . . He sleeps; but he is awakened; he opens his eyes; behold, the horrid thing stands at his bedside . . . On the morrow I announced that I had thought of a story. I began that day with the words, 'It was on a dreary night of November' . . ."

3   Walter Scott, *Blackwood's Edinburgh Magazine*, 1818. "It is no slight merit in our eyes, that the tale, though wild in incident, is written in plain and forcible English, without exhibiting that mixture of hyperbolical Germanisms with which tales of wonder

are usually told . . . The ideas of the author are always clearly as well as forcibly expressed; and his descriptions of landscape have in them the choice requisites of truth, freshness, precision, and beauty. The self-education of the monster, considering the slender opportunities of acquiring knowledge that he possessed, we have already noticed as improbable and overstrained. That he should have not only learned to speak, but to read, and, for aught we know, to write . . . seems as unlikely . . ."

4 *The Literary Panorama and National Register*, 1818. "We have mentioned that there are gross inconsistencies in the minor details of the story . . . the moment Frankenstein has endowed with life the previously inanimate form of the being which he has made, he is so horror-struck . . . while the gigantic monster runs from the horizontal posture in which he lay, and *walks away* . . . The author supposes that his hero has the power of communicating *life* to dead matter: but what has the vital principle to do with *habits* . . . it would no more have been able to *walk* without having previously acquired the *habit* of doing so, than it would be to talk, or to reason, or to judge . . . The whole detail of the development of the creature's mind and faculties is full of these monstrous inconsistencies . . . and learns to talk and read thro' a chink in the wall!

5 *The Edinburgh Magazine and Literary Miscellany*, 1818. "There never was a wilder story imagined, yet, like most of the fictions of this age, it has an air of reality attached to it . . . The real events of the world have, in our day, too, been of so wondrous and gigantic a kind . . . that Shakespeare himself, in his wildest flights, has been completely distanced by the eccentricities of actual existence . . . Our appetite . . . for every sort of wonder and vehement interest, has in this way become so desperately inflamed . . . we can be satisfied with nothing in fiction that is not highly

coloured and exaggerated . . . our greatest inventors, accordingly, have been obliged to accommodate themselves to the taste of the age, more, we believe, than their own judgment can, at all times, have approved of . . ."

6 John Wilson Croker, *Quarterly Review*. ". . . a tissue of horrible and disgusting absurdity this work presents . . . striking language of the insane, and the author . . . leaves us in doubt whether he is not as mad as his hero . . . Frankenstein has passages which appal the mind and make the flesh creep, we have given it all the praise (if praise it can be called) which we dare to bestow . . . will not even amuse its readers, unless their taste have been deplorably vitiated . . ."

7 *The British Critic*, 1818. ". . . writings of this extravagant character . . . bear marks of considerable power . . . but this power is so abused and perverted, that we should almost prefer imbecility . . . these volumes have neither principle, object, nor moral; the horror which abounds in them is too grotesque and *bizarre* ever to approach near the sublime, and when we did not hurry over the pages in disgust, we sometimes paused to laugh outright . . . The writer of it is, we understand, a female; this is an aggravation of that which is the prevailing fault of the novel; but if our authoress can forget the gentleness of her sex, it is no reason why we should; and we shall therefore dismiss the novel without further comment."

8 Author's Introduction, 1831. ". . . I shall thus give a general answer to the question, so very frequently asked of me—'How I, then a young girl, came to think of and to dilate upon so very hideous an idea?'"

9 Authors Introduction, 1831 edition. "At first I thought but a few pages—of a short tale; but Shelley urged me to develope the idea at greater length. I certainly did not owe

the suggestion of one incident, nor scarcely of one train of feeling, to my husband . . ."

10 Letter I. ". . . as I walk in the streets of Peterburgh, I feel a cold northern breeze play upon my cheeks, which braces my nerves, and fills me with delight. Do you understand this feeling? This breeze, which has traveled from the regions toward which I am advancing, gives me a fore-taste of those icy climes . . . Six years have passed since I resolved on my present undertaking . . . They fly quickly over the snow in their sledges . . . The cold is not exces-sive; if you are wrapped in furs . . . I have no ambition to lose my life on the post-road between St Peterburgh and Archangel."

11 Letter I. ". . . the sun is forever visible . . . I may there dis-cover the wondrous power which attracts the needle . . . may tread a land never before imprinted by the foot of man . . . discovering a passage near the pole to those countries . . . This expedition has been the favorite dream of my early years . . . and when shall I return? . . . If I succeed, many, many months, perhaps years, will pass before you and I may meet. If I fail, you will see me again soon, or never."

12 Letter II: Archangel, March 28th 17—. "How slowly time passes here, encompassed as I am by frost and snow! . . . I have hired a vessel, and am occupied in collecting my sailors . . . I have no friend, Margaret: when I am glow-ing with the enthusiasm of success, there will be none to participate my joy; if I am assailed by disappointment, no one will endeavor to sustain me in dejection . . . You may deem me romantic . . . Well, these are useless complaints; I shall certainly find no friend on the wide ocean . . . my voyage is only now delayed until the weather shall permit my embarkation."

13 Letter II. "Remember me with affection, should you never hear from me again." Letter 3. ". . . floating sheets of ice that continually pass us . . . We have already reached a very high latitude . . . No incidents have hitherto befallen us that would make a figure in a letter . . . Thus far I have gone, tracing a secure way over pathless seas . . ."

14 Letter IV. "So strange an accident has happened to us that I cannot forbear recording it . . . we were nearly surrounded by ice, which closed in the ship on all sides . . . when a strange sight suddenly attracted our attention . . . We perceived a low carriage, fixed on a sledge and drawn by dogs, pass on towards the north, at the distance of half a mile; a being which had the shape of a man, but apparently of gigantic stature, sat in the sledge, and guided the dogs . . . We were, as we believed, many hundred miles from any land; but this apparition seemed to denote that it was not, in realty, so distant as we had supposed."

15 Letter IV. "About two hours after this occurrence we heard the ground sea; and before night the ice broke, and freed our ship . . . In the morning, however, as soon as it was light, I went upon deck and found all the sailors busy on one side of the vessel, apparently talking to some one in the sea. It was, in fact, a sledge, like that we had seen before, which had drifted towards us in the night on a large fragment of ice . . . the stranger addressed me in English, although with a foreign accent. 'Before I come on board your vessel,' said he, 'will you have the kindness to inform me whither you are bound?' . . . I replied, however, that we were on a voyage of discovery towards the northern pole . . . Upon hearing this he appeared satisfied, and consented to come on board . . . His limbs were nearly frozen, and his body dreadfully emaciated by fatigue and suffering."

16 Letter IV. ". . . he asked a multitude of questions concerning the route which the daemon, as he called him, had

pursued . . . He is now much recovered from his illness, and is continually on the deck, apparently watching for the sledge that preceded his own . . . the paroxysm of grief that had seized the stranger overcame his weakened powers . . . he appeared to despise himself for being a slave to passion . . . 'I have lost everything and cannot begin life anew . . . I have suffered great and unparalleled misfortunes . . . I imagine that you may deduce an apt moral from my tale . . ."

17 Chapter I. "I am by birth a Genevese, and my family is one of the most distinguished of that republic. My ancestors had been for many years counselors and syndics, and my father had filled several public situations. with honour and reputation. He was respected by all who knew him, for his integrity and indefatigable attention to public business." Chapter II. "No human being could have passed a happier childhood than myself."

18 Chapter I. "As the circumstances of [my father's] marriage illustrate his character, I cannot refrain from relating them. One of his most intimate friends was a merchant who, from a flourishing state, fell, through numerous mischances, into poverty . . . [the merchant] retreated with his daughter to the town of Lucerne . . . The interval was, consequently, spent in inaction; his grief only became more deep and rankling . . . her father died in her arms, leaving her an orphan and beggar . . . Two years after this event Caroline became [my father's] wife. There was a considerable difference between the ages of my parents . . ."

19 Chapter I. "I remained for several years their only child. Much as they were attached to each other, they seemed to draw inexhaustible stores of affection from a very mine of love to bestow them upon me. My mother's tender caresses and my father's smile of benevolent pleasure while regarding me, are my first recollections. I was their

plaything and their idol . . . I was so guided by a silken cord that all seemed but one train of enjoyment to me."

20　Chapter I. ". . . immediately after their union they sought the pleasant climate of Italy . . . From Italy they visited Germany and France . . . I, their eldest child, was born at Naples, and as an infant accompanied them in their rambles . . . My mother had much desire to have a daughter . . . When I was about five years old . . . they passed a week on the shores of the Lake Como. Their benevolent disposition often made them enter the cottages of the poor . . . She found a peasant and his wife . . . distributing a scanty meal to five hungry babes . . . Among these there was one which attracted my mother far above all the rest. She appeared of a different stock. The four others were dark-eyed, hardy little vagrants; this child was thin, and very fair. Her hair was the brightest living gold . . ."

21　Chapter I. ". . . my mother prevailed on her rustic guardians to yield their charge to her . . . On the evening previous to her being brought to my home, my mother said playfully, —'I have a pretty present for my Victor—tomorrow he shall have it.' And when, on the morrow, she presented Elizabeth to me as her promised gift, I, with childish seriousness, interpreted her words literally and looked upon Elizabeth as mine—mine to protect, love, and cherish . . . We called each other familiarly by the name cousin . . . till death she was to be mine only."

22　Chapter II. "[Elizabeth] busied herself with following the aerial creations of the poets; and in the majestic and wondrous scenes which surrounded our Swiss home—the sublime shapes of the mountains; the changes of the seasons . . . We possessed a house in Geneva, and a *campagne* on Belrive, the eastern shore of the lake . . . the closest friendship to one among them. Henry Clerval . . . He tried to make us act plays and to enter into masquerades, in which the characters were drawn from . . . the Round Table of King Arthur . . . My parents were possessed by the very spirit of kindness and indulgence . . . When I mingled with other families, I distinctly discerned how peculiarly fortunate my lot was . . . It was the secrets of heaven and earth that I desired to learn . . . the metaphysical, or in its highest sense, the physical secrets of the world."

23 Chapter II. "Natural philosophy is the genius that has regulated my fate . . . I chanced to find a volume of the works of Cornelius Agrippa . . . If . . . my father had taken the pains to explain to me that the principles of Agrippa had been entirely exploded, and that a modern system of science had been introduced . . . my ideas would never have received the fatal impulse that led to my ruin . . . I read and studied the wild fancies of these writers with delight . . . a fervent longing to penetrate the secrets of nature . . . I entered with the greatest diligence into the search of the philosopher's stone and the elixir of life . . . if I could banish disease from the human frame and render man invulnerable to any but a violent death! . . . The raising of ghosts or devils was a promise liberally accorded by my favorite authors . . ."

24 Chapter II. ". . . till an accident again changed the current of my ideas . . . a most violent and terrible thunder-storm . . . a stream of fire issued from an old and beautiful oak . . . the oak had disappeared, and nothing remained but a blasted stump . . . reduced to thin ribbons of wood . . . the explanation of a theory which he had formed on the subject of electricity and galvanism . . . I at once gave up my former occupations . . . I betook myself to mathematics, and the branches of study appertaining to that science . . ."

25 Chapter III. "When I had attained the age of seventeen, my parents resolved, that I should become a student at the university of Ingolstadt . . . My departure was therefore fixed

at an early date; but, before the day resolved upon could arrive, the first misfortune of my life occurred . . . Elizabeth had caught the scarlet fever . . . Elizabeth was saved, but the consequences of this imprudence were fatal to her preserver. On the third day my mother sickened . . . She died calmly . . . [Elizabeth] indeed veiled her grief, and strove to act the comforter of us all . . . She devoted herself to those whom she had been taught to call her uncle and cousins."

26 Chapter III. ". . . as I proceeded, my spirits and hopes rose. I ardently desired the acquisition of knowledge . . . paid a visit to some of the principal professors . . . led me first to M. Krempe, professor of natural philosophy . . . I replied carelessly; and, partly in contempt, mentioned the names of my alchymists . . ."

27 Chapter III. "The professor stared. 'Have you,' he said, 'really spent your time in studying such nonsense?.. every instant that you have wasted on those books is utterly and entirely lost. You have burdened your memory with exploded systems and useless names. Good god! In what desert land have you lived, where no one was kind enough to inform you that these fancies which you have so greedily imbibed are a thousand years old and as musty as they are ancient? I little expected, in this enlightened and scientific age, to find a disciple of Albertus Magnus and Paracelus. My dear sir, you must begin your studies entirely anew.'"

28 Chapter III. "I returned home, not disappointed, for I have said that I had long considered those authors useless whom the professor reprobated . . . Besides, I had a contempt for the uses of modern natural philosophy . . . I went into the lecture room, which M. Waldman entered shortly after. This professor was very unlike his colleague . . . with an aspect expressive of the greatest benevolence . . . he concluded with a panegyric upon modern chemistry, the terms of which I shall never forget . . ."

29 Chapter III. "'The ancient teachers of this science,' said '[Waldman], 'promised impossibilities, and performed nothing. The modern masters promise very little . . . whose hands seem only made to dabble in dirt, and their eyes to pore over the microscope or crucible, have indeed performed miracles . . . they have discovered how the blood circulates, and the nature of the air we breathe' . . ."

30 Chapter III. "He heard with attention the little narration concerning my studies, and smiled at the names of Cornelius Agrippa and Paracelsus, but without the contempt that M. Krempe had exhibited. He said that 'these were men to whose indefatigable zeal modern philosophers were indebted for most of the foundations of their knowledge . . . The labours of men of genius, however erroneously directed, scarcely ever fail in ultimately turning to the solid advantage of mankind . . . If your wish is to become really a man of science, and not merely a petty experimentalist, I should advise you to apply to every branch of natural philosophy, including mathematics.'"

31 Chapter IV. "From this day natural philosophy, and particularly chemistry, in the most comprehensive sense of the term, became nearly my sole occupation . . . Two years passed in this manner, during which I paid no visit to Geneva, but was engaged, heart and soul, in the pursuit of some discoveries which I hoped to make . . . When, I often asked myself, did the principle of life proceed? It was a bold question . . . and determined thenceforth to apply myself more particularly to those branches of natural philosophy which relate to physiology . . . I became acquainted with the science of anatomy . . ."

32 Chapter IV. "To examine the causes of life, we must first have recourse to death . . . I must also observe the natural decay and corruption of the human body . . . a churchyard was to me merely the receptacle of bodies deprived of life,

which, from being the seat of beauty and strength, had become food for the worm . . . Now I was led to examine the cause and progress of this decay, and forced to spend days and nights in vaults and charnel-houses . . . I saw how the worm inherited the wonders of the eye and brain."

33 Chapter IV. ". . . from the midst of this darkness a sudden light broke in upon me—a light so brilliant and wondrous, yet so simple . . . I was surprised, that among so many men of genius who had directed their enquiries towards the same science, that I alone should be reserved to discover so astonishing a secret . . . After days and nights of incredible labour and fatigue, I succeeded in discovering the cause of generation and life; nay, more. I became myself capable of bestowing animation upon lifeless matter . . . I see by your eagerness and the wonder and hope which your eyes express, my friend, that you expect to be informed of the secret with which I am acquainted; that cannot be . . . how dangerous is the acquirement of knowledge . . ."

34 Chapter IV. "When I found so astonishing a power placed within my hands, I hesitated a long time concerning the manner in which I should employ it. Although I possessed the capacity of bestowing animation, yet to prepare a frame for the reception of it, with all its intricacies of fibres, muscles, and veins, still remained a work of inconceivable difficulty and labour. I doubted at first whether I should attempt the creation of a being like myself, or one of simpler organization; but my imagination was too much exalted by my first success to permit me to doubt of my ability to give life to an animal as complex and wondrous as man . . . I began the creation of a human being . . . As the minuteness of the parts formed a great hindrance to my speed, I resolved, contrary to my first intention, to make the being of a gigan-

tic stature; that is to say, about eight feet in height, and proportionately large."

35 Chapter IV. "A new species would bless me as its creator and source . . . No father could claim the gratitude of his child so completely as I should deserve theirs . . . if I could bestow animation upon lifeless matter, I might in process of time . . . renew life where death had apparently devoted the body to corruption. These thoughts supported my spirits, while I pursued my undertaking with unremitted ardour. My cheek had grown pale with study, and my person had become emaciated with confinement."

36 Chapter IV. ". . . the moon gazed on my midnight labours . . . Who shall conceive the horrors of my secret toil as I dabbled among the unhallowed damps of the grave, or tortured the living animal to animate lifeless clay? . . . a resistless, and almost frantic impulse, urged me forward; I seemed to have lost all soul or sensation but for this one pursuit . . . The dissecting room and the slaughter-house furnished many of my materials . . ."

37 Chapter IV. "In a solitary chamber, or rather cell, at the top of the house, and separated from all the other apartments by a gallery and staircase, I kept my workshop of filthy creation . . . Winter, spring, and summer passed away during my labours; but I did not watch the blossom or the expanding leaves . . . Every night I was oppressed by a slow fever, and I became nervous to a most painful degree; the fall of a leaf startled me, and I shunned my fellow-creatures as if I had been guilty of a crime."

38 Chapter IV. "And the same feelings which made me neglect the scenes around me caused me also to forget those friends who were so many miles absent . . . If the study to which you apply yourself has a tendency to weaken your affections, and to destroy your taste for those simple

pleasures in which no alloy can possibly mix, then that study is certainly unlawful . . . if no man allowed any pursuit whatsoever to interfere with the tranquility of his domestic affections, Greece had not been enslaved; Ceasar would have spared his country; America would have been discovered more gradually; and the empires of Mexico and Peru had not been destroyed."

39 Chapter V. "It was on a dreary night of November, that I beheld the accomplishment of my toils . . . I collected the instruments of life around me, that I might infuse the spark of being into the lifeless thing that lay at my feet. It was already one in the morning; the rain pattered dismally against the panes, and my candle was nearly burnt out, when, by the glimmer of the half-extinguished light, I saw the dull yellow eye of the creature open; it breathed hard, and a convulsive motion agitated my limbs. How can I describe my emotions at this catastrophe . . ."

40 Chapter V. ". . . or how delineate the wretch whom with such infinite pains, and care I had endeavored to form? . . . His yellow skin scarcely covered the work of muscles and arteries beneath; his hair was of a lustrous black, and flowing . . . straight black lips . . ."

41 Chapter V. "I had worked hard for nearly two years, for the sole purpose of infusing life into an inanimate body. For this I had deprived myself of rest and health . . . but now that I had finished, the beauty of the dream vanished, and breathless horror and disgust filled my heart. Unable to endure the aspect of the being I had created, I rushed out of the room . . . I threw myself on the bed in my clothes . . . I slept, indeed, but I was disturbed by the wildest dreams."

42 Chapter V. "I thought I saw Elizabeth . . . as I imprinted the first kiss on her lips, they became livid with the hue of death . . . I held the corpse of my dead mother in my arms;

a shroud enveloped her form, and I saw the grave-worms crawling in the fold of flannel. I started from my sleep with horror . . ."

43 Chapter V. ". . . [the monster] forced its way through the widow shutters, I beheld the wretch—the miserable monster whom I had created. He held up the curtain of the bed; and his eyes, if eyes they may be called, were fixed on me. His jaws opened, and he muttered some inarticulate sounds, while a grin wrinkled his cheeks . . . one hand was stretched out, seemingly to detain me, but I escaped, and rushed downstairs. I took refuge in the courtyard belonging to the house . . . I remained during the rest of the night, walking up and down in the greatest agitation . . . I issued into the streets, pacing them with quick steps . . ."

44 Chapter V. "I did not dare return to the apartment . . . I continued walking in this manner for some time, endeavoring by bodily exercise to ease the load that weighed upon my mind . . . not daring to look about me: 'Like one, on a lonesome road who, / Doth walk in fear and dread, / And, having once turned round, walks on, / And turns no more his head; / Because he knows a frightful fiend / Doth close behind him tread*' . . . *Coleridge's Ancient Mariner . . . my eyes fixed on a coach that was coming towards me from the other end of the street . . . it stopped just where I was standing; and, on the door being opened, I perceived Henry Clerval who, on seeing me, instantly sprung out."

45 Chapter V. "Nothing could equal my delight on seeing Clerval . . . the thought made me shiver, that the creature whom I had left in my apartment might still be there, alive and walking about. I dreaded to behold this monster; but I feared still more that Henry should see him. Intreating him, therefore, to remain a few minutes at the bottom of the stairs, I darted up towards my own room."

Appendix

46 Chapter V. "I threw the door forcibly open, as children are accustomed to do when they expect a spectre to stand in waiting for them on the other side; but nothing appeared. I stepped fearfully in: the apartment was empty; and my bedroom was also freed from its hideous guest. I could hardly believe that so great a good fortune could have befallen me . . ."

47 Chapter V. "I clapped my hands for joy and ran down to Clerval. We ascended into my room, and the servant presently brought breakfast; but I was unable to contain myself . . . I jumped over the stairs, clapped my hands, and laughed aloud . . . my loud, unrestrained, heartless laughter . . ."

48 Chapter V. "Clerval continued talking for some time about our mutual friends and his own good fortune in being permitted to come to Ingolstadt . . . 'to undertake a voyage of discovery to the land of knowledge . . . My dear Victor,' cried [Henry], 'what, for God's sake, is the matter? Do not laugh in that manner. How ill you are! What is the cause of all this?'"

49 Chapter V. "This was the commencement of a nervous fever, which confined me for several months. During all that time Henry was my only nurse . . . The form of the monster on whom I had bestowed existence was forever before my eyes, and I raved incessantly concerning him . . . By very slow degrees, and with frequent relapses that alarmed and grieved my friend, I recovered . . . in a short time I became as cheerful a before I was attached by the fatal passion."

50 Chapter V. "'You will repay me entirely, if you do not discompose yourself, but get well as fast as you can; and since you appear in such good spirits, I may speak to you on one subject, may I not?'"

51 Chapter V. "I trembled. One subject! What could it be? Could he allude to an object on whom I dared not even think?"

52 Chapter V. ". . . 'your father and cousin would be very happy if they received a letter from you in your own handwriting. They hardly know how ill you have been, and are uneasy at your long silence.'"

53 Chapter V. "'Is that all my dear Henry? How could you suppose that my first thought would not fly towards those dear, dear friends whom I love, and who are so deserving of my love?' 'If that is your present temper, my friend, you will perhaps be glad to see a letter that has been lying here some days for you: it is from your cousin, I believe.'"

54 Chapter VI. "Clerval then put the following letter into my hands. It was from my own Elizabeth: My dearest cousin . . . Clerval writes that indeed you are getting better I eagerly hope that you will confirm this intelligence soon in your own handwriting . . ."

55 Chapter VI. "Little alteration, except the growth of our dear children, has taken place since you left us. The blue lake, and snow-clad mountains—they never change; and I think our placid home and our contented hearts are regulated by the same immutable laws."

56 Chapter VI. "How pleased you would be to remark the improvement of our Ernest! He is now sixteen, and full of activity and spirit. He is desirous to a true Swiss, and to enter the foreign service . . . My uncle is not pleased with the idea of a military career in a distant country, but Ernest never had your powers of application. He looks upon study as an odious fetter; his time is spent in the open air, climbing the hills or rowing on the lake."

57 Chapter VI. "Do you remember on what occasions Justine Moritz entered our family? Probably you do not . . . Madame Mortiz, her mother, was a widow with four children . . . when Justine was twelve years of age, prevailed on her mother to allow her to live at our house . . . Justine, you may remember, was a great favourite of yours . . . One by one, her brothers and sister died . . . [Justine] is very clever and gentle, and extremely pretty . . ."

58 Chapter VI. ". . . darling William . . . he is very tall for his age, with sweet laughing blue eyes, dark eyelashes, and curling hair. When he smiles, two little dimples appear on each cheek, which are rosy with health. He has already had one or two little wives, but Louisa Biron is his favourite, a pretty little girl of five years of age."

59 Chapter VI. "The pretty Miss Mansfield has already received the congratulatory visits on her approaching marriage with a young Englishman . . . Her ugly sister, Manon, married M. Duvillard, the rich banker, last autumn . . . Your favourite school-fellow, Louis Manoir, has suffered misfortunes . . . But he has already recovered his spirits and is reported to be on the point of marrying a very lively, pretty Frenchwoman . . . must older than Manoir; but she is very much admired . . . My trifling occupations take up my time and amuse me . . . Write, dearest Victor—one line—one word will be a blessing . . . I, intreat you, write!"

60 Chapter VI. "'Dear, dear Elizabeth!' I exclaimed, when I had read her letter, 'I will write instantly, and relieve them from the anxiety they must feel.' I wrote . . . When I was otherwise quite restored to health, the sight of a chemical instrument would renew all agony of my nervous symptoms . . ."

61 Chapter VI. "[Henry] had also changed my apartment . . . Summer passed away in these occupations, and my return

to Geneva was fixed for latter end of autumn; but being delayed by several accidents, winter and snow arrived, the roads were deemed impassable, and my journey was retarded until the ensuing spring."

62 Chapter VII: ". . . I found the following letter from my father . . . William is dead! . . . he is murdered! . . . Last Thursday (May 7th) I, my niece, and your two brothers went to walk in Plainpalais . . . we discovered that William and Ernest, who had gone on before, were not to be found . . . Presently Ernest came . . . William had run away to hide himself . . . we continued to search for him until night fell . . . I discovered my lovely boy, whom the night before I had seen blooming and active in health, stretched on the grass livid and motionless: the print of the murder's finger was on his neck . . ."

63 Chapter VII: "William had teased [Elizabeth] to let him wear a very valuable miniature that she possessed of your mother. The picture is gone, and was doubtless the temptation which urged the murderer to the deed . . . Come, dearest Victor; you alone can console Elizabeth. She weeps continually and accuses herself unjustly as the cause of his death . . ."

64 Chapter VII. "I passed through scenes familiar to my youth, but which I had not seen for nearly six years . . . Fear overcame me; I dared not advance . . . I remained two days in Lausanne . . . I resolved to visit the spot where my poor William had been murdered. As I could not pass through the town, I was obliged to cross the lake in a boat to arrive at Plainpalais. During this short voyage I saw the lightnings playing on the summit of Mont Blanc in the most beautiful figures . . . The storm, as is often the case in Switzerland, appeared at once in various parts of the heavens . . . I wandered on with hasty step."

Appendix

65 Chapter VII. "I clasped my hands and exclaimed aloud, 'William, dear angel! This is thy funeral, this thy dirge!' As I said these words, I perceived in the gloom a figure which stole from behind a clump of trees near me . . . A flash of lightning illuminated the object, and discovered its shape plainly to me; its gigantic stature, and the deformity of its aspect, more hideous than belongs to humanity . . . it was the wretch, the filthy daemon to whom I had given life. What did he there? Could he be (I shuddered at the conception) the murderer of my brother? No sooner did that idea cross my imagination than I became convinced of its truth . . ."

66 Chapter VII. "The figure passed me quickly, and I lost it in the gloom . . . *He* was the murderer! . . . another flash discovered him to me hanging among the rocks of the nearly perpendicular ascent of Mont Salêve . . . He soon reached the summit, and disappeared . . . Alas! I had turned loose into the world a depraved wretch, whose delight was in carnage and misery, had he not murdered my brother?"

67 Chapter VII. "No one can conceive the anguish I suffered during the remainder of the night, which I spent, cold and wet, in the open air . . . Day dawned; and I directed my steps towards town . . . My first thought was to discover what I knew of the murderer, and cause instant pursuit to be made. But I paused when I reflected on the story that I had to tell. A being whom I myself had formed, and endued with life, had met me at midnight among the precipices of an inaccessible mountain. I remembered also the nervous fever with which I had been seized just at the time that I dated my creation, and which would give an air of delirium to a tale otherwise so utterly improbable. Who could arrest a creature capable of scaling the overhanging sides of Mont Salêve?"

68 Ibid.

69 Chapter VII. "'Ernest entered: he had heard me arrive, and hastened to welcome me. He expressed a sorrowful delight to see me. 'Welcome, my dearest Victor,' said he. 'Ah! I wish you had come three mongths ago . . . your persuasions will induce Elizabeth to cease her vain and tormenting self-accusations . . . She most of all,' said Ernest, 'requires consolation, she accused herself of having caused the death of my brother, and that made her very wretched. But since the murderer has been discovered—' . . ."

70 Chapter VII. "'The murderer discovered! Good God! how can that be? who could attempt to pursue him? It is impossible; one might as well try to overtake the winds or confine a mountain-stream with a straw. I saw him too; he was free last night.'"

71 Chapter VII. "'I do not know what you mean,' replied my brother, in accents of wonder, 'but to us the discovery we have made completes our misery. No one would believe at first; and even now Elizabeth will not be convinced, notwithstanding all the evidence. Indeed, who would credit that Justine Moritz, who was so amiable and fond of all the family, could suddenly become capable of so frightful, so appalling a crime?'"

72 Chapter VII. ". . . 'several circumstances came out that have almost forced conviction upon us; and her own behavior has been so confused as to add to the evidence of facts . . . the morning on which the murder of poor William had been discovered, Justine had been taken ill . . . one of the servants, happening to examine the apparel she had worn on the night of the murder, had discovered in her pocket the picture of my mother, which had been judged to be the temptation of the murderer.'"

73 Chapter VII. "'Justine Moritz! Poor, poor girl, is she the accused? But it is wrongfully; everyone knows that . . .

You are all mistaken' . . . I had no fear, therefore, that any circumstantial evidence could be brought forward strong enough to convict her. My tale was not one to announce publicly; its astounding horror would be looked upon as madness by the vulgar . . . 'She is innocent, my Elizabeth' . . ."

74 Chapter VIII. "The trial began . . . Several strange facts combined against her, which might have staggered any one who had not such proof of her innocence as I had. She had been out the whole of the night on which the murder had been committed, and towards morning was perceived by a market-woman not far from the spot where the body of the murdered child had been afterwards found. The woman asked her what she did there; but she looked very strangely, and only returned a confused and unintelligible answer . . . When shown the body, she fell into violent hysterics, and kept her bed for several days."

75 Chapter VIII. "'God knows,' [Justine] said, 'how entirely I am innocent.' She then related . . . she had passed the night on which the murder had been committed at the house of an aunt at Chêne . . . On her return, at about nine o'clock, she met a man who asked her if she had seen any thing of the child who was lost. She was alarmed by this account, and passed several hours looking for him, when the gates of Geneva were shut . . ."

76 Chapter VIII. ". . . she was forced to remain several hours of the night in a barn belonging to a cottage, being unwilling to call up the inhabitants, to whom she was well known. Most of the night she spent here watching; towards morning she believed that she slept for a few minutes; some steps disturbed her, and she awoke . . . again endeavor to find my brother . . . Concerning the picture she could give no account . . . 'Did the murderer place it there? I know of no opportunity for him doing so' . . ."

77 Chapter VIII: "Several witnesses were called . . . Elizabeth . . . desired permission to address the court . . . A murmur of approbation followed Elizabeth's simple and powerful appeal; but it was excited by her generous interference, and not in favour of poor Justine, on whom the public indignation was turned with renewed violence . . . the popular voice and the countenances of the judges had already condemned my unhappy victim . . . The ballots had been thrown; they were all black, and Justine was condemned."

78 Chapter VIII. ". . . Justine had already confessed her guilt . . . This was strange and unexpected intelligence . . . a dire blow to Elizabeth, who had relied with firmness upon Justine's innocence . . . 'Oh, Justine!' said [Elizabeth], 'why did you rob me of my last consolation? I relied on your innocence . . . I believed you guiltless, notwithstanding every evidence, until I heard that you had yourself declared your guilt . . . [Victor] is more convinced of your innocence than I was . . .'"

79 Chapter VIII. "'I did confess; but I confessed a lie. I confessed, that I might obtain absolution . . . Ever since I was condemned, my confessor has besieged me; he threatened and menaced, until I almost began to think that I was the monster that he said I was. He threatened excommunication and hell fire in my last moments if I continued obdurate . . . Dear William! dearest blessed child! I soon shall see you again in heaven . . .'"

80 Chapter VIII. "Could the daemon who had . . . murdered my brother also in his hellish sport have betrayed the innocent to death and ignominy? . . . I could not answer . . . And on the morrow Justine died . . . She perished on the scaffold as a murderess! . . . William and Justine, the first hapless victims to my unhallowed arts."

81 Chapter IX. "I was seized by remorse and the sense of guilt . . . My father observed with pain the alteration

perceptible in my disposition and habits, and endeavored by arguments, deduced from the feelings of his serene conscience and guiltless life; to inspire me with fortitude, and awaken in me the courage to dispel the dark cloud which brooded over me . . . I ardently wished to extinguish that life which I had so thoughtlessly bestowed . . . my hatred and revenge burst all bounds of moderation . . . Elizabeth was sad . . . eternal woe and tears she then thought was the just tribute she should pay to innocence so blasted and destroyed . . . Elizabeth read my anguish in my countenance, and kindly taking my hand, said, 'My dearest friend, you must calm yourself . . . revenge, in your countenance makes me tremble. Dear Victor, banish these dark passions.'"

82 Chapter IX. "Often, after the rest of the family had retired for the night, I took the boat and passed many hours upon the water. Sometimes, with my sails set, I was carried by the wind . . . I lived in daily fear lest the monster whom I had created should perpetrate some new wickedness. I had an obscure feeling that all was not over, and that he would still commit some signal crime . . . bending my steps towards the near Alpine valleys, sought in the magnificence, the eternity fo such scenes, to forget myself and my ephemeral, because human, sorrows . . ." Chapter X. ". . . we are moved by every wind that blows and a chance word or scene that that word may convey to us. We rest; a dream has power to poison sleep. / We rise; one wand'ring thought pollutes the day. / We feel . . ."

83 Chapter X. "I resolved to ascend to the summit of Montanvert . . . I descended upon the glacier . . . the vast river of ice, wound among its dependent mountains, whose aerial summits hung over its recesses. Their icy and glittering peaks shone in the sunlight over the clouds. My heart,

which was before sorrowful, now swelled with something like joy . . ."

84 Chapter X. ". . . I suddenly beheld the figure of a man, at some distance, advancing towards me with superhuman speed . . . his stature, also, as he approached, seemed to exceed that of a man . . . it was the wretch whom I had created . . . 'Devil," I exclaimed, '. . . Begone, vile insect!' . . . My rage was without bounds; I sprang on him, impelled by all the feelings which can arm one being against the existence of another. He easily eluded me . . ."

85 Chapter X. "'Be calm! I intreat you to hear me, before you give vent to your hatred on my devoted head . . . Life, although it may only be an accumulation of anguish, is dear to me, and I will defend it. Remember, thou hast made me more powerful than thyself; my height is superior to thine, my joints more supple.'"

86 Chapter X. "I was troubled: a mist came over my eyes, and I felt a faintness seize me . . . 'do you dare approach me? . . . stay, that I may trample you to dust! . . . come on, then, that I may extinguish the spark which I so negligently bestowed . . .'"

87 Chapter X. "'I expected this reception,' said the daemon . . . 'How dare you sport thus with life? Do your duty toward me, and I will do mine towards you and the rest of mankind. If you will comply with my conditions, I will leave them and you at peace; but if you refuse, I will glut the maw of death, until it be satiated with the blood of your remaining friends . . . Hear my tale; it is long and strange, and the temperature of this place is not fitting to your fine sensations; come to the hut upon the mountain.'"

88 Chapter XI. "'It is with considerable difficulty that I remember the original era of my being: all the events of that period appear confused and indistinct . . . it was, indeed,

a long time before I learned to distinguish the operation of my various senses. By degrees, I remember, a stronger light pressed upon my nerves, so that I was obliged to shut my eyes. Darkness then came over me . . . The light become more and more oppressive to me . . . I sought a place where I could receive shade. This was the forest near Ingolstadt . . . I ate some berries . . . I slaked my thirst at the brook . . .'"

89 Chapter XI. "'I felt cold also . . . Before I had quitted your apartment, on a sensation of cold, I had covered myself with some clothes . . . under one of the trees I found a huge cloak, with which I covered myself . . . Several changes of day and night passed, and the orb of night had greatly lessened.'"

90 Chapter XI. "'. . . on all sides various scents saluted me . . . I began to distinguish my sensations from each other . . . I was delighted when I first discovered that a pleasant sound, which often saluted my ears, proceeded from the throats of the little winged animals . . . Sometimes I tried to imitate the pleasant songs of the birds, but was unable . . . I found a fire which had been left by some wandering beggars, and was overcome with delight at the warmth . . . I found some of the offals that the travellers had left had been roasted, and tasted much more savoury . . .'"

91 Chapter XI. "'. . . at length I perceived a small hut . . . And old man sat in it, near a fire, over which he was preparing breakfast. He turned on hearing a noise; and perceiving me, shrieked loudly, and quitting the hut, ran across the fields with a speed of which his debilitated form hardly appeared capable.'"

92 Chapter XI. "'I greedily devoured the remnants of the shepherd's breakfast, which consisted of bread, cheese, milk, and wine . . . overcome by fatigue, I lay down among

some straw, and fell asleep . . . at sunset I arrived at a village. How miraculous did this appear! the huts, the neater cottages, and stately houses engaged my admiration by turns . . . One of the best of these I entered; but hardly I had placed my foot within the door before the children shrieked, and one of the women fainted. The whole village was roused; some fled, some attacked me, until, grievously bruised by stones and many other missile weapons . . .'"

93 Ibid.

94 Chapter XI. "'. . . I escaped to the open country and fearfully took refuge in a low hovel . . . This hovel, however, joined a cottage of a neat and pleasant appearance . . . it was dry . . . a paradise compared to the bleak forest . . . a small and almost imperceptible chink, through which the eye could just penetrate. Through this crevice a small room was visible . . . What chiefly struck me was the gentle manner of these people . . .' Chapter XII. "'The young man was constantly employed out of doors, and the girl in various laborious occupation within. The old man, whom I soon perceived to be blind . . .'"

95 Chapter XI. "'. . . she returned bearing the pail, which was now partly filled with milk . . . the old man, who, taking up an instrument, began to play, and to produce sounds sweeter . . . some roots and plants, which she placed in water, and then upon the fire . . . the young man went into the garden, and appeared busily employed in digging and pulling up roots . . . '" Chapter XII. "'A considerable period elapsed before I discovered one of the causes of the uneasiness of this amiable family: it was poverty . . . Their nourishment consisted entirely of the vegetables of their garden and the milk of one cow . . . They often, I believe, suffered the pangs of hunger very poignantly . . . they placed food before the old man when they reserved

none for themselves. This trait of kindness moved me sensibly . . . the youth spent a great part of each day collecting wood for the family fire . . .'"

96 Chapter XII. "'. . . I longed to join them, but dared not . . . I found that these people possessed a method of communicating their experience and feelings to one another by articulate sounds. I perceived that the words they spoke sometimes produced pleasure or pain . . . I discovered the names that were given to some of the most familiar objects of discourse . . . I learned the ideas appropriated to each of these sounds, and was able to pronounce them.'"

97 Chapter XII. "'. . . during the night I often took his tools, the use of which I quickly discovered, and brought home firing sufficient for the consumption of several days . . . how was I terrified, when I viewed myself in a transparent pool! . . . I was in reality the monster that I am, I was filled with the bitterest sensations of despondence and mortification. Alas! I did not yet entirely know the fatal effects of this miserable deformity.'"

98 Chapter XI. "'. . . I felt sensations of a peculiar and overpowering nature: they were a mixture of pain and pleasure, such as I had never before experienced . . . I withdrew from the window, unable to bear these emotions.'" Chapter XII. "'. . . these labours, performed by an invisible hand, greatly astonished them; and once or twice I heard them, on these occasions, utter the words 'good spirit,' 'wonderful' . . . I was inquisitive to know why Felix appeared so miserable and Agatha so sad . . . I looked upon them as superior beings, who would be the arbiters of my future destiny.'"

99 Chapter XIII. "'It was a lady on horseback . . . of angelic beauty and expression. Her hair of a shining raven black . . . she held out her hand to Felix, who kissed it rapturously

and called her, as well as I could distinguish, his sweet Arabian . . . "sweet Safie" . . . '" Chapter XIV. "'. . . I learned the history of my friends . . .'"

100 Citation lost.

101 Chapter XIV. "'. . . the old man was DeLacey. He was descended from a good family in France, where he had lived for many years in affluence . . . they had lived in a large and luxurious city called Paris . . . The father of Safie had been the cause of their ruin. He was a Turkish merchant . . .'"

102 Chapter XIV. "'. . . seized and cast into prison . . . condemned to death . . . his religion and wealth rather than the crime alleged against him had been the cause . . . Felix had accidentally been present at the trial . . . He made, at that moment, a solemn vow to deliver him . . . [Felix] saw the lovely Safie . . . the captive possessed a treasure which would fully reward his toil and hazard.'"

103 Ibid.

104 Chapter XIV. "'Felix had procured passports in the name of his father, sister, and himself . . . [his father] aided the deceit . . . Felix conducted the fugitives through France to Lyons and across Mont Cenis to Leghorn . . . The Turk allowed this intimacy to take place, and encouraged the hopes of the youthful lovers, while in his heart he had formed far other plans . . . The government of France were greatly enraged at the escape . . . DeLacey and Agatha were thrown into prison . . . [the Turk] quitted Italy with his daughter, insultingly sending Felix a pittance of money to aid him . . .'"

105 Chapter XIV. "'They remained confined for five months before the trial took place; the result of which deprived them of their fortune and condemned them to a perpetual

exile . . . a miserable asylum in the cottage in Germany, where I discovered them . . . Safie resolved in her own mind the plan of conduct . . . took care that Safie should arrive in safety at the cottage of her lover.'"

106 Chapter XIII. "'The book from which Felix instructed Safie was Volney's *Ruins of Empires* . . . I obtained a cursory knowledge of history . . . the manners, governments, and religions of the different nations of the earth . . . For a long time I could not conceive how one man could go forth to murder his fellow . . . I heard of the division of property, of immense wealth and squalid poverty; of rank, descent, and noble blood . . . I cannot describe to you the agony that these reflections inflicted upon me . . . Of what strange nature is knowledge . . . I wished sometimes to shake off all thought and feeling; but I learned that there was but one means to overcome the sensation of pain, and that was death . . . '" Chapter XV. "'I can hardly describe to you the effect of these books. They produced in me an affinity of new images and feelings, that sometimes raised me to ecstasy, but more frequently sunk me into the lowest dejection . . . disquisitions on death and suicide . . . The winter advanced, and an entire revolution of the seasons had taken place since I awoke into life.'"

107 Chapter XV. "'I discovered some papers in the pocket of the dress which I had taken from your laboratory . . . It was your journal of the four months that preceded my creation . . . the minutest description of my odious and loathsome person is given, in language which painted your own horrors, and rendered mine indelible. I sickened as I read. 'Hateful day when I received life!' I exclaimed in agony. 'Accursed creator! . . . a monster so hideous that even *you* turned from me in disgust?'"

108 Chapter V. ". . . the demoniacal corpse . . . A mummy again endued with animation could not be so hideous as that

wretch . . . it became a thing such as even Dante could not have conceived . . ." Chapter XV. " . . . Satan had his companions, fellow-devils, to admire and encourage him; but I am solitary and abhorred.'"

109 Chapter XV. ". . . I contemplated the virtues of the cottagers, their amiable and benevolent dispositions, I persuaded myself that when they should become acquainted with my admiration of their virtues, they would compassionate me and overlook my personal deformity . . . The presence of Safie diffused happiness among its inhabitants . . ."

110 Chapter XV. "One day . . . Safie, Agatha, and Felix departed on a long country walk . . . this was the hour and moment of trial . . . I knocked. 'Who is there?' said the old man—'Come in.' I entered . . . 'By your language, stranger, I suppose you are my countryman;—are you French?' . . . 'To be friendless is indeed to be unfortunate' . . . 'they behold only a monster.'

111 Chapter XV. "'From your lips first have I heard the voice of kindness directed towards me; I shall be forever grateful' . . . At that instant the cottage door was opened, and Felix, Safie, and Agatha entered. Who can describe their horror and consternation on beholding me? Agaitha fainted; and Safie, unable to attend to her friend, rushed out of the cottage. Felix darted forward, and with supernatural force tore me from his father . . . he dashed me to the ground and struck me violently with a stick . . . overcome by pain and anguish, I quitted the cottage . . ." Chapter XVI. ". . . wandered in the wood; and now . . . gave vent to my anguish in fearful howlings."

112 Chapter XVI. ". . . wished to tear up the trees, spread havoc and destruction around me . . . from that moment I declared ever-lasting war against the species, and, more than all, against him who had formed me . . . I could not

help believing that I had been too hasty in my conclusions
. . . I resolved to return to the cottage, seek the old man,
and by my representations win him to my party . . . The
inside of the cottage was dark, and I heard no motion . . .
I never saw any of the family of De Lacey more . . . anger
returned, a rage of anger . . . I placed a variety of combus-
tibles around the cottage . . . The wind fanned the fire, and
the cottage was quickly enveloped by the flames . . ."

113 Chapter XVI. ". . . whither should I bend my steps? . . . I
learned from your papers that you were my father, my creator . . . You had mentioned Geneva as the name of your
native town . . . From only you could I hope for succour,
although towards you I felt no sentiment but that of hatred.
Unfeeling, heartless creator! . . . But on you only had I any
claim for pity and redress, and from you I determined to
seek that justice which I vainly attempted to gain from any
other being that wore the human form . . . My travels were
long . . ."

114 Chapter XVI. ". . . when I arrived on the confines of Switzerland . . . I generally rested during the day, and travelled
only when I was secured by night from the view of man . . .
One morning, however . . . the day . . . cheered even me
by the loveliness of its sunshine . . . forgetting my solitude
and deformity, dared to be happy . . . a young girl came
running towards the spot where I was concealed . . . her
foot slipt, and she fell into the rapid stream . . . I rushed
from my hiding place, and, with extreme labour from the
force of the current, saved her, and dragged her to shore
. . . On seeing me, he darted towards me, and tearing the
girl from my arms . . . he aimed a gun . . . and fired . . . This
was then the reward of my benevolence! . . . The ball had
entered my shoulder . . ."

115 Chapter XVI. ". . . I reached the environs of Geneva. It
was evening when I arrived . . . the approach of a beauti-

ful child . . . 'You are an ogre—Let me go, or I will tell my papa . . . My papa is a Syndic—he is M. Frankenstein—he will punish you.' . . . 'Frankenstein! you belong then to my enemy—to him towards whom I have sworn eternal revenge; you shall be my first victim.' . . . I grasped his throat to silence him, and in a moment he lay dead at my feet . . . I gazed on my victim, and my heart swelled with exultation and hellish triumph . . ."

116 Chapter XVI. ". . . I saw something glittering on his breast. I took it; it was a portrait of a most lovely woman . . . my rage returned: I remembered that I was forever deprived of the delights that such beautiful creatures could bestow . . . I entered a barn which had appeared to me to be empty. A woman was sleeping on some straw . . . not I, but she, shall suffer; the murder I have committed because I am forever robbed of all that she could give me, she shall atone . . . I bent over her and placed the portrait securely in one of the folds of her dress."

117 Chapter XVI. "For some days I haunted the spot where these scenes had taken place; sometimes wishing to see you . . . consumed by a burning passion which you alone can gratify. We may not part until you have promised to comply with my requisition. I am alone, and miserable; man will not associate with me; but one as deformed and horrible as myself would not deny herself to me. My companion must be of the same species, and have the same defects. This being you must create." Chapter XVII. "You must create a female for me . . . and I demand it . . ."

118 Chapter XVII. "'I do refuse it,' I replied . . . 'Shall I create another like yourself, whose joint wickedness might desolate the world? Begone! I have answered you; you may torture me, but I will never consent.'"

119 Ibid.

Appendix

120 Chapter XVII. "'You are in the wrong,' replied the fiend . . .
'I am content to reason with you. I am malicious because
I am miserable. Am I not shunned and hated by all mankind? You, my creator, would tear me to pieces . . . I will
revenge my injuries; if I cannot inspire love, I will cause
fear, and chiefly towards you my arch-enemy, because my
creator, do I swear inextinguishable hatred. Have a care: I
will work at your destruction, nor finish until I desolate your
heart, so that you shall curse the hour of your birth . . . This
passion is detrimental to me; for you do not reflect that *you*
are the cause of its excess . . .'"

121 Ibid.

122 Chapter XVII. "'Our lives will not be happy, but they will be
harmless . . . Oh! my creator, make me happy . . . If you
consent, neither you nor any other human being shall ever
see us again: I will go to the vast wilds of South America.
My food is not that of man . . . acorns and berries afford me
sufficient nourishment . . . We shall make our bed of dried
leaves.'"

123 Chapter XVII. "'How can you . . . persevere in this exile?'
. . . After a long pause of reflection, I concluded that the
justice due both to him and my fellow creatures demanded
of me that I should comply with his request . . . 'I consent to
your demand, on your solemn oath to quit Europe forever,
and every other place in the neighborhood of man . . .'"

124 Chapter XVII. "'I swear,' he cried . . . 'Depart to your home,
and commence your labours: I shall watch their progress
with unutterable anxiety; and fear not but that when you
are ready I shall appear.' Saying this, he suddenly quitted
me, fearful, perhaps of any change in my sentiments."

125 Ibid.

126 Chapter XVII. "I saw him descend the mountain with greater speed than the flight of an eagle . . . my heart was heavy, and my steps slow . . ." Chapter XVIII. "I found that I could not compose a female without again devoting several months to profound study and laborious disquisition."

127 Chapter XVIII. "I had heard of some discoveries having been made by an English philosopher, the knowledge of which was material to my success . . . 'I confess, my son, that I have always looked forward to your marriage with our dear Elizabeth' . . . I expressed a wish to visit England; but concealing the true reasons of this request . . . Without previously communicating with me, [my father] had, in concert with Elizabeth, arranged that Clerval should join me . . . it was understood that my union with Elizabeth should take place immediately on my return . . . During my absence I should leave my friends unconscious of the existence of their enemy, and unprotected from his attacks, exasperated as he might be by my departure. But he had promised to follow me wherever I might go . . . my chemical instruments should be packed to go with me."

128 Ibid.

129 Chapter XVIII. "We had agreed to descend the Rhine in a boat from Strasburgh to Rotterdam, whence we might take shipping for London . . . The river descends rapidly, and winds between hills, not high, but steep, and of beautiful forms. We saw many ruined castles . . . flourishing vineyards . . . we proceeded by sea to England . . . saw the white cliffs of Britain."

130 Chapter XIX. "London was our present point of rest; we determined to remain several months in this wonderful and celebrated city . . . I was principally occupied with the means of obtaining the information necessary for the completion of my promise . . . I now also began to collect the

materials necessary for my new creation . . . we received a letter from a person in Scotland . . . We accordingly determined to commence our journey towards the north . . ."

131 Chapter XVIII. "The delight of Clerval was proportionately greater than mine . . . His feelings are forever on the stretch; and when he begins to sink into repose, he finds himself obliged to quit that on which he rests in pleasure for something new, which again engages his attention, and which also he forsakes for new novelties . . . I had now neglected my promise for some time, and I feared the effects of the daemon's disappointment . . . This idea pursued me, and tormented me at every moment from which I might otherwise have snatched repose and peace . . . I was in no mood to laugh and talk with strangers . . ."

132 Chapter XIX. "I packed up my chemical instruments and the materials I had collected, resolving to finish my labours in some obscure nook in the northern highlands of Scotland . . . I told Clerval that I wished to make the tour of Scotland alone . . . fixed on one of the remotest of the Orkneys as the scene of my labours . . . hardly more than a rock . . . On the whole island there were but three miserable huts, and one of these was vacant when I arrived. This I hired . . . In this retreat I devoted the morning to labour . . ."

133 Chapter XIX. ". . . as I proceeded in my labour, it became every day more horrible and irksome to me . . . It was, indeed, a filthy process in which I was engaged. During my first experiment, a kind of enthusiastic frenzy had blinded me to the horror of my employment . . . But now I went to it in cold blood, and my heart often sickened at the work of my hands."

134 Chapter XIX. "Every moment I feared to meet my persecutor. Sometimes I sat with my eyes fixed on the ground,

fearing to raise them . . . I worked on, and my labour was already considerably advanced." Chapter XX ". . . I should leave my labour for the night, or hasten its conclusion by an unremitting attention . . . a train of reflection occurred to me, which led me to consider the effects of what I was now doing."

135 Chapter XX. "I was now about to form another being, of whose dispositions I was alike ignorant; she might become ten thousand times more malignant than her mate . . . They might even hate each other; the creature who already lived loathed his own deformity . . . She also might turn with disgust from him to the superior beauty of man; she might quit him . . ."

136 Chapter XX. ". . . one of the first results of those sympathies for which the daemon thirsted would be children, and a race of devils would be propagated upon the earth, who might make the very existence of the species of man a condition precarious and full of terror . . . the wickedness of my promise burst upon me; I shuddered to think that future ages might curse me as their pest . . ."

137 Chapter XX. "I trembled, and my heart failed within me, when, on looking up, I saw, by the light of the moon, the daemon at the casement. A ghastly grin wrinkled his lips . . . his countenance expressed the utmost extent of malice and treachery . . . trembling with passion, [I] tore to pieces the thing on which I was engaged. The wretch saw me destroy the creature on whose future existence he depended for happiness and, with a howl of devilish despair and revenge, withdrew."

138 Chapter XX. "I left the room, and, locking the door, made a solemn vow in my own heart never to resume my labours . . . I sought my own apartment. I was alone . . . Several hours passed, and I remained near my window gazing on

the sea . . . my ear was suddenly arrested by the paddling of oars near the shore, and a person landed close to my house . . . I heard the creaking of my door, as if some one endeavored to open it softly . . . the wretch whom I dreaded appeared."

139 Chapter XX. "'You have destroyed the work which you began; what is it that you intend? Do you dare break your promise? I have endured toil and misery . . . I crept along the shores of the Rhine, among its willow islands . . . I have dwelt many months in the heaths of England, and among the deserts of Scotland. I have endured incalculable fatigue, and cold, and hunger; do you dare destroy my hopes?'"

140 Chapter XX. "'You are my creator, but I am your master;— obey! . . . you, my tyrant and tormentor, shall curse the sun that gazes on your misery.. I will watch with the wiliness of a snake, that I may sting with its venom . . . I go; but remember, I shall be with you on your wedding-night.'"

141 Chapter XX. "'Begone! I do break my promise; never will I create another like yourself, equial in deformity and wickedness . . . Shall I, in cool blood, set looseupon the earth a daemon, whose delight is in death and wretchedness? . . . Villian! before you sign my death warrant, be sure that you are yourself safe' . . . I thought again of his words— *'I will be with you on your wedding-night.'* That then was the period fixed for the fulfillment of my destiny. In that hour I should die . . ."

142 Chapter XX. ". . . in a few moments I saw him in his boat, which shot across the waters with an arrowy swiftness . . . Why had I not followed him, and closed with him in mortal strife? But I had suffered him to depart, and he had directed his course towards the main land . . ."

143 Chapter XX. "The remains of the half-finished creature, whom I had destroyed, lay scattered on the floor, and I almost felt as if I had mangled the living flesh of a human being . . . I accordingly put them into a basket, with a great quantity of stones . . ."

144 Chapter XX. "I had been awake the whole of the preceding night . . . Between two and three in the morning the moon rose . . . aboard a little skiff, sailed out about four miles from the shore . . . cast my basket into the sea . . . fixing the rudder in a direct position, stretched myself at the bottom of the boat . . . in a short time I slept soundly."

145 ChapterXX. ". . . when I awoke I found that the sun had already mounted considerably . . . I felt a few sensations of terror. I had no compass with me.. so slenderly acquainted with the geography of this part of the world . . . I might be driven into the wide Atlantic . . . the sea, it was to be my grave. 'Fiend,' I exclaimed, 'your task I already fulfilled!' . . . suddenly I saw a line of high land towards the south . . . steered my course towards the land . . . resolved to sail directly towards the town . . . several people crowded towards the spot."

146 Chapter XX. "'My good friends,' said I, 'will you be so kind as to tell me the name of this town, and inform me where I am?' . . . 'You will know soon enough,' replied a man with a hoarse voice. 'May be you are come to a place that will not prove much to your taste; but you will not be consulted as to your quarters, I promise you.' I was exceedingly surprised on receiving so rude an answer . . . 'it is the custom of the Irish to hate villains . . . ' '. . . you are to give an account of the death of a gentleman who was found murdered here last night.'"

147 Chapter XXI. ". . . one being selected by the magistrate, he deposed, that he had been out fishing the night before . . .

they found that he had fallen on the body of a man, who was to all appearance dead . . . the clothes were not wet . . . the body was not cold . . . the black mark of fingers on his neck."

148 Chapter XXI. "I entered the room where the corpse lay, and was led up to the coffin. How can I describe my sensations of beholding it? . . . the lifeless form of Henry Clerval stretched before me . . . I exclaimed, 'Have my murderous machinations deprived you also, my dearest Henry, of life?' . . . The human frame could no longer support the agonies that I endured, and I was carried out of the room in strong convulsions . . ."

149 Chapter XXI. "I lay for two months on the point of death, my ravings, as I afterwards heard, were frightful . . . Why did I not die? . . . Of what materials was I made, that I could resist so many shocks, which, like the turning of the wheel, continually renewed the torture? But I was doomed to live; and, in two months, found myself as awaking from a dream, in a prison . . ."

150 Chapter XIX. ". . . Mr. Kirwin entered. His countenance expressed sympathy and compassion . . . 'you will, I hope, soon quit this melancholy abode; for, doubtless, evidence can easily be brought to free you from this criminal charge . . . some one, a friend, is come to visit you . . .'"

151 Chapter XXI ". . . in a moment my father entered . . . 'What a place is this that you inhabit, my son!' said he, looking mournfully at the barred windows, and wretched appearance of the room. 'You traveled to seek happiness, but a fatality seems to pursue you. And poor Clerval' . . . My father was enraptured on finding me freed from the vexations of a criminal charge . . . and permitted to return to my native country."

152 Chapter XXI. ". . . 'some destiny of the most horrible kind hangs over me, and I must live to fulfil it' . . . The cup of life was poisoned forever; and although the sun shone upon me, as upon the happy and gay of heart, I saw around me nothing but a dense and frightful darkness, penetrated by no light but the glimmer of two eyes that glared upon me . . . the watery, clouded eyes of the monster . . . We took our passage on board a vessel . . ."

153 Chapter XXI. "Ever since my recovery from the fever, I had been in the custom of taking every night a small quantity of laudanum . . . I now swallowed double my usual quantity . . . But sleep did not afford me respite . . . my dreams presented a thousand objects that scared me . . . I was possessed by a kind of nightmare . . ." Chapter XXII. "We landed, and proceeded to Paris . . . 'I am the assassin of those most innocent victims; they died by my machinations' . . . this speech convinced my father that my ideas were deranged . . ."

154 Chapter XXII. ". . . I received the following letter from Elizabeth: . . . 'It gave me the greatest pleasure to receive a letter from my uncle dated at Paris, you are no longer at a formidable distance, and I may hope to see you in less than a fortnight. My poor cousin, how much you must have suffered! . . . I would not disturb you at this period, when so many misfortunes weigh upon you, but a conversation . . . renders some explanation necessary before we meet. Explanation! You may possible say . . . do you love another? . . . I could not help supposing that you might regret our connection . . . I love you . . . do not answer tomorrow, or the next day . . . if I see but one smile on your lips when we meet . . . I shall need no other happiness.'"

155 Ibid.

156 Ibid.

Appendix

157 Chapter XXII. ". . . I wrote to Elizabeth . . . 'I fear, my beloved girl,' I said. 'little happiness remains for us on earth; yet all that I may one day enjoy is centred in you . . . ."

158 Chapter XXII. "I have one secret, Elizabeth, a dreadful one; when revealed to you, it will chill your frame with horror, and then, far from being surprised at my misery, you will only wonder that I survive what I have endured. I will confide this tale of misery and terror to you the day after our marriage . . ."

159 Chapter XXII. ". . . we returned to Geneva . . . my father spoke of my immediate marriage with Elizabeth. I remained silent . . . the remembrance of the threat returned . . . *'I shall be with you on your wedding-night,'* I should regard the threatened fate as unavoidable. But death was no evil to me, if the loss of Elizabeth were balanced with it . . ."

160 Chapter XXII. "I carried pistols and a dagger constantly about me . . . But on the day that was to fulfill my wishes and my destiny, she was melancholy, and a presentiment of evil pervaded her; and perhaps also she thought of the dreadful secret, which I had promised to reveal to her on the following day . . ."

161 Chapter XXII. "'You are sorrowful, my love. Ah! if you knew what I have suffered, and what I may yet endure, you would endeavor to let me taste the quiet and freedom from despair that this one day at least permits me to enjoy.'"

162 Chapter XXII. "'be assured that if a lively joy is not painted in my face, my heart is contented. Something whispers to me not to depend too much on the prospect that is opened before us, but I will not listen to such a sinister voice . . . the dome of Mont Blanc, render this scene of beauty . . . Look also at the innumerable fish that are swimming in the clear waters, where we can distinguish every pebble that lies at

the bottom. What a divine day! how happy and serene all nature appears!'"

163 Ibid.

164 Chapter XXII. "After the ceremony was performed, a large party assembled at my father's; but it was agreed that Elizabeth and I should commence our journey by water . . ." Chapter XXIII. ". . . [we] retired to the inn, and contemplated the lovely scene of waters, woods, and mountains, obscured in darkness . . . Suddenly a heavy storm of rain descended . . . a thousand fears arose in my mind . . . my right hand grasped a pistol . . . I would sell my life dearly, and not shrink from the conflict . . ."

165 Chapter XXIII. ". . . suddenly I reflected how fearful the combat which I momentarily expected would be to my wife, and I earnestly intreated her to retire, resolving not to join her until I had obtained some knowledge as to the situation of my enemy."

166 Chapter XXIII. "She left me, and I continued some time walking up and down the passages of the house, and inspecting every corner that might afford a retreat to my adversary. But I discovered no trace of him . . . suddenly I heard a shrill and dreadful scream . . . It came from the room into which Elizabeth had retired. As I heard it, the whole truth rushed into my mind . . ."

167 Chapter XXIII. ". . . I rushed into the room. Great God! . . . the purest creature of earth? She was there, lifeless and inanimate, thrown across the bed, her head hanging down . . . The murderous mark of the fiend's grasp was on her neck . . ."

168 Chapter XXIII. "I saw at the open window a figure a figure the most hideous and abhorred. A grin was on the face of the monster; he seemed to jeer, as with his fiendish finger

he pointed towards the corpse of my wife. I rushed towards the window, and drawing a pistol from my bosom, fired; but he eluded me, leaped from his station, and, running with the swiftness of lightning, plunged into the lake."

169 Chapter XXIII. "The report of the pistol brought a crowd into the room . . . we followed the track with boats; nets were cast, but in vain . . . [I] crawled into the room where the corpse of my beloved lay . . . I hung over it, and joined my sad tears to theirs . . . no creature had ever been so miserable as I was . . ."

170 Chapter XXIII. ". . . my father even now might be writhing under his grasp, and Ernest might be dead at his feet. This idea made me shudder, and recalled me to action . . . I must return by the lake; but the wind was unfavourable . . . I hired men to row . . . Mine has been a tale of horrors . . . Know that, one by one, my friends were snatched away; I was left desolate . . . I arrived at Geneva. My father and Ernest yet lived; but the former sunk under the tidings that I bore . . . in a few days he died in my arms."

171 Ibid.

172 Chapter XXIII. ". . . why did I not then expire? . . . Alas! life is obstinate, and clings closest where it is most hated . . . I awoke, and found myself in a dungeon . . . was then released from my prison. For they had called me mad; and during many months, as I understood, a solitary cell had been my habitation . . ."

173 Chapter XXIII. ". . . after my release, I repaired to a criminal judge in the town, and told him that I had an accusation to make . . . I now related my history . . . The magistrate appeared at first perfectly incredulous . . . He endeavored to soothe me as a nurse does a child, and reverted my tale as the effects of delirium." Chapter XIV. ". . . I found myself

at the entrance of the cemetery where William, Elizabeth, and my father reposed."

174 Chapter XIV. "Every thing was silent, except the leaves of the trees . . . They were dead, and I lived; their murderer also lived . . . with quivering lips exclaimed, 'By the sacred earth on which I kneel . . . I swear . . . to pursue the daemon, who caused this misery, until he or I shall perish in mortal conflict. For this purpose I will preserve my life: to execute this dear revenge' . . . Let the cursed and hellish monster drink deep of agony . . . I was answered through the stillness of night by a loud and fiendish laugh."

175 Ibid.

176 Chapter XXIV. "'I am satisfied: miserable wretch! you have determined to live, and I am satisfied.'"

177 Chapter XIV. "I have traversed a vast portion of the earth . . . I pursued him . . . Guided by a slight clue, I followed the windings of the Rhône, but vainly. The blue Mediterranean appeared . . ."

178 Chapter XXIV. ". . . by a strange chance, I saw the fiend enter by night, and hide himself in a vessel bound for the Black Sea . . . Amidst the wilds of Tartary and Russia . . . Sometimes the peasants, scared by his horrid apparition, informed me of his path; sometimes he himself . . . left some mark to guide me . . ."

179 Chapter XXIV. ". . . I was cursed by some devil . . . yet still a spirit of good followed . . . overcome by hunger, sunk under exhaustion, a repast was prepared for me in the desert . . . parched by thirst, a slight cloud would bedim the sky, shed the few drops that revived me, and vanish."

180 Chapter XXIV. ". . . during sleep alone that I could taste joy. O blessed sleep! . . . in sleep I saw my friends, my wife, and my beloved country . . . my father . . . Clerval . . .

I persuaded myself that I was dreaming until night should come, and that I should then enjoy reality in the arms of my dearest friends . . ."

181 Chapter XXIV. "Sometimes, indeed, he left marks in writing on the barks of the trees, or cut in stone, that guided me, and instigated my fury. 'My reign is not yet over' . . . 'you live, and my power is complete. Follow me; I seek the everlasting ices of the north, where you will feel the misery of cold and frost, to which I am impassive. You will find near this place, if you follow not too tardily, a dead hare; eat, and be refreshed. Come on, my enemy; we have yet to wrestle for our lives; but many hard and miserable hours must you endure until that period shall arrive . . . Prepare! your toils only begin; wrap yourself in furs, and provide food, for we shall soon enter upon a journey where your sufferings will satisfy my everlasting hatred.'"

182 Ibid.

183 Ibid.

184 Chapter XXIV. "Scoffing devil! Again do I vow vengeance; again do I devote thee, miserable fiend, to torture and death. Never will I give up my search, until he or I perish; and then with what ecstasy shall I join my Elizabeth and my departed friends . . ."

185 Chapter XXIV. ". . . the snows thickened, and the cold increased in a degree almost too severe to support . . . The rivers were covered with ice . . . I had procured a sledge and dogs . . . I now gained on him . . . he was but one day's journey in advance . . ."

186 Chapter XXIV. ". . . at a wretched hamlet on the sea shore. I enquired of the inhabitants . . . A gigantic monster, they said, had arrived the night before, armed with a gun and many pistols . . . He had carried off their store of winter

food, and, placing it on a sledge . . . had pursued his journey across the sea in a direction that led to no land . . ."

187 Chapter XXIV. "I departed from land. I cannot guess how many days have passed since then; but I have endured misery . . . three weeks in this journey . . . I behld my enemy at no more than a mile distant . . . A ground sea was heard . . . the sea roared . . . it split, and cracked . . . I was left drifting on a scattered piece of ice . . . several of my dogs died . . . I saw your vessel riding at anchor . . . I quickly destroyed part of my sledge to construct oars . . . I had determined if you were going southward, still to trust myself to the mercy of the seas rather than abandon my purpose."

188 Ibid.

189 Chapter XXIV. ". . . must I die, and yet he live? If I do, swear to me, Walton, that he shall not escape, that you will seek him, and satisfy my vengeance in his death . . . He is eloquent and persuasive . . . trust him not . . . call on the manes of William, Justine, Clerval, Elizabeth, my father, and of the wretched Victor, and thrust your sword into his heart."

190 Chapter XXIV. "You have read this strange and terrific story, Margaret . . . like a volcano bursting forth . . . [Frankenstein] shrieked out imprecations on his persecutor . . ."

191 Chapter XXIV. ". . . the letter of Felix and Safie, which he showed me, and the apparition of the monster seen from our ship, brought to me greater conviction of the truth . . . I endeavored to gain from Frankenstein the particulars of his creature's formation . . ."

192 Chapter XXIV. "'Are you mad, my friend?' said he; 'or whither does your senseless curiosity lead you? Would you also create for yourself and the world a demoniacal

enemy? Peace, peace! learn from my miseries, and do not seek to increase your own.'"

193 Chapter XXIV. "'When younger,' said he, 'I believed myself destined for some great enterprise . . . I possessed a coolness of judgement that fitted me for illustrious achievements . . . the work I had completed, no less a one than the creation of a sensitive and rational animal . . . now serves only to plunge me lower in the dust . . . I am chained to an eternal hell. My imagination was vivid, yet my powers of analysis and application were intense . . . I conceived the idea, and executed the creation of a man . . . I trod heaven in my thoughts, now exulting in my powers . . . I was imbued with high hopes and lofty ambition; but how I am sunk!'"

194 Ibid.

195 Chapter XXIV. "You have read this strange and terrific story, Margaret . . . Our conversations are not always confined to his own history and misfortunes. On every point of general literature he displays unbounded knowledge, and a quick and piercing apprehension. His eloquence is forcible and touching . . . What a glorious creature must he have been in the days of his prosperity, when he is thus noble and godlike in ruin! He seems to feel his own worth, and the greatness of his fall . . . I write to you, encompassed by peril, and ignorant whether I am ever doomed to see again dear England . . . I am surrounded by mountains of ice, which admit no escape, and threaten every moment to crush my vessel . . . If we are lost, my mad schemes are the cause . . . I almost dread a mutiny caused by this despair."

196 Chapter XXIV. "The cold is excessive, and many of my unfortunate comrades have already found a grave amidst this scene desolation. Frankenstein has daily declined in

health . . . This morning . . . I was roused by half a dozen of the sailors, who demanded admission to the cabin . . . to make me a requisition, which, in justice, I could not refuse . . . if the vessel should be freed I would instantly direct my course southward."

197 Chapter XXIV. "What do you mean? What do you demand of your captain? Are you then so easily turned from your design? Did you not call this a glorious expedition? . ∴. And now, behold, with the first imagination of danger . . . you shrink away . . . poor souls, they were chilly and returned to their warm firesides . . . ye need not have come thus far, and dragged your captain to the shame of a defeat . . . This ice is not made of such stuff as your heart may be; it is mutable, and cannot withstand you . . ."

198 Chapter XXIV. "During these last days I have been occupied in examining my past conduct; nor do I find it blameable. In a fit of enthusiastic madness I created a rational creature, and was bound towards him, to assure, as far as was in my power, his happiness and well-being. This was my duty; but there was another still paramount to that. My duties toward the beings of my own species had greater claims to my attention, because they included a greater proportion of happiness or misery. Urged by this view, I refused, and I did right in refusing, to create a companion for the first creature. He showed unparalleled malignity and selfishness, in evil; he destroyed my friends; he devoted to destruction beings who possessed exquisite sensations, happiness, and wisdom; nor do I know where this thirst for vengeance may end. Miserable himself, that he may render no other wretched, he ought to die. The task of his destruction was mine, but I have failed."

199 Chapter XXIV. "'Do you then really return? . . . Do so, if you will; but I will not. You may give up your purpose, but mine is assigned to me by heaven, and I dare not. I am

weak; but surely the spirits who assist my vengeance will endow me sufficient strength . . . my judgment and ideas are already disturbed by the near approach of death . . . I may still be misled by passion . . . Seek happiness in tranquility, and avoid ambition, even if it be only the apparently innocent one of distinguishing yourself in science and discoveries. Yet why do I say this? I have myself been blasted in these hopes, yet another may succeed.'"

200 Chapter XXIV. "How all this will terminate, I know not; but I had rather die than return shamefully,—my purpose unfulfilled. Yet I fear such will be my fate; the men, unsupported by ideas of glory and honour, can never willingly continue to endure their present hardships. September 7th. The die is cast; I have consented to return, if we are not destroyed. Thus are my hopes blasted by cowardice and indecision: I come back ignorant and disappointed. It requires more philosophy than I possess, to bear this injustice with patience. September 12th. It is past; I am returning to England . . . the ice began to move . . . the passage towards the south became perfectly free . . ."

201 Chapter XXIV. "[Frankenstein] pressed my hand feebly, and his eyes closed for ever, while the irradiation of a gentle smile passed away from his lips. Margaret, what coment can I make on the untimely extinction of this glorious spirit? . . . My tears flow, my mind is overshadowed by a cloud of disappointment . . . I am interrupted . . . there is a sound as of a human voice, but hoarser; it comes from the cabin where the remains of Frankenstein still lie."

202 Chapter XXIV. "Great God! what a scene has just taken place! . . . I entered the cabin where lay a form which I cannot find words to describe:—gigantic in stature, yet uncouth and distorted in its proportions. As he hung over the coffin, his face was concealed by long locks of ragged hair; but one vast hand was extended, in colour and

apparent texture like that of a mummy. When he heard the sound of my approach, he ceased to utter exclamations of grief and horror, and sprung towards the window. Never did I behold a vision so horrible as his face, of such loathsome, yet appalling hideousness . . . I called on him to stay."

203 Chapter XXIV. "'That is also my victim,' [the monster] exclaimed; 'in his murder my crimes are consummated; the miserable series of my being is wound to its close! Oh, Frankenstein! generous and self-devoted being! what does it avail that I now ask thee to pardon me? I, who irretrievably destroyed thee by destroying all thou lovedst.'"

204 Chaper XXIV. ". . . 'do you think that I was then dead to agony and remorse? . . . he suffered not in the consummation of the deed;—oh! not the ten-thousandth portion of the anguish that was mine during the lingering detail of its execution. A frightful selfishness hurried me on, while my heart was poisoned with remorse. Think you that the groans of Clerval were music to my ears? My heart was fashioned to be susceptible of love and sympathy; and when wrenched by misery to vice and hatred, it did not endure the violence of the change, without torture such as you cannot even imagine . . . I abhorred myself . . . but I was the slave, not the master, of an impulse, which I detested, yet could not disobey . . . And now it is ended; there is my last victim! The fallen angel becomes a malignant devil . . . I desired love and fellowship, and I was still spurned. Was there no injustice in this? Am I to be thought the only criminal, when all human kind sinned against me? . . . My work is nearly complete.'"

205 Ibid.

206 Chapter XXIV. "Do not think that I shall be slow to perform this sacrifice. I shall quit your vessel on the ice-raft

which brought me thither, and shall seek the most north-ern extremity of the globe; I shall collect my funeral pile, and consume to ashes this miserable frame . . . I shall die . . . I shall no longer see the sun or stars, or feel the winds play on my cheeks . . . Farewell! I leave you, and in you the last of human-kind whom these eyes will ever behold. Farewell, Frankenstein! . . . Blasted as thou wert, my agony was still superior to thine; for the bitter sting of remorse will not cease to rankle in my wounds until death shall close them for ever . . . I shall ascend my funeral pile triumphantly, and exult in the agony of the torturing flames. The light of that conflagration will fade away; my ashes will be swept into the sea by the winds . . . . Farewell."

207 Ibid.

208 Ibid.